Sacred Hunger

The Vampire in Myth and Reality

by Michelle Belanger

AF472620

Dark Moon Press ❖ Fort Wayne, IN

Sacred Hunger is published by Dark Moon Press
Fort Wayne, Indiana

For a full catalogue of Dark Moon's publications, refer to:
http://www.darkmoonpress.net
Or send an SASE to:
P.O. Box 11496, Fort Wayne, Indiana 46858-1496

Cover design by Michelle Belanger
Cover photograph by Pendragon Photography © 2005
Models: Michelle Belanger and Penumbra
Inside design by Michelle Belanger, with design
elements by Carol Belanger Grafton

"The Lord of Vampires" first appeared in the January 2005 issue of *Fate Magazine* and is reprinted with kind permission.

Sacred Hunger is © Michelle Belanger, 2005

All rights reserved. No part of this book my be reproduced in part or whole in any format whatsoever without first contacting the author for permission. Exemption is granted to reviewers and researchers for the quotation of short excerpts of up to one hundred words in the length for the purpose of critical analysis or review.

To contact the author, please refer to her official website:
http://www.michellebelanger.com

Or send an SASE to:
Michelle Belanger, PO Box 1120, Brunswick, OH 44212 USA

Other works by Michelle Belanger:

Darksong: Fantasies in Twilight (Shadowfox, 1994)
The Enchanted Wood (Shadowfox, 1996)
The Vampyre Almanc 2000 (with Father Sebastian)
The Psychic Vampire Codex (Weiser, 2004)
Soul Songs from Distant Lands (Emerald Tablet, 2005)
Fallen Angel Rhapsody (Emerald Tablet, 2005)

Forthcoming:
These Haunted Dreams (Dark Moon, 2006)
Necromancy: the Forbidden Art (2006)
The Psychic Energy Book (Weiser, 2006)
Lifting the Black Veil (2006)

Table of Contents

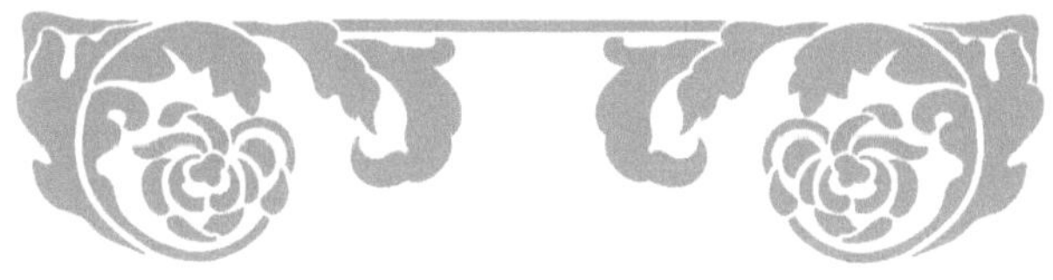

Photo Credits

PENDRAGON PHOTOGRAPHY © 2004-5:

Detail from "My Nightmare," Don Henrie, p. 11
"Blood is the Life," Don Henrie, p. 15
"The Devil's Sonata, " Don Henrie, p. 26
"The Accused," Don Henrie, p. 31
"Loss of Innocence," Don Henrie and Laura Dark, p. 39
"Shadow of the Dead," Don Henrie and Laura Dark, p. 53
"Cavalier," Don Henrie, p. 58
"Byronic," Michelle Belanger, p. 62
"Sacred Hunger," Michelle Belanger and Penumbra, p. 70
"Virginal," Penumbra, p. 76
"Dark Angel," Don Henrie and Laura Dark, p. 84
"Leanan-Sidhe," Kitty, p. 90
"Lord Vampire," Don Henrie with Jezebel, Kitty, Lilith, Makayla, Michelle, and Penumbra, p. 105
"Vamp," Michelle Belanger and Jasmyn DuBois, p. 112
"Dark Passions," Michelle Belanger and Makyala, p. 118
"Evil Eye," Don Henrie and Michelle Belanger, Lilith, Makayla, and Kitty, p. 123
"Decadence," Don Henrie, p. 130

TOM TRAINER STUDIOS © 1994, 2005

"Masquerade," Michelle Belanger and Matthias, p. 43
"Kiss of Death," Michelle Belanger, p. 50

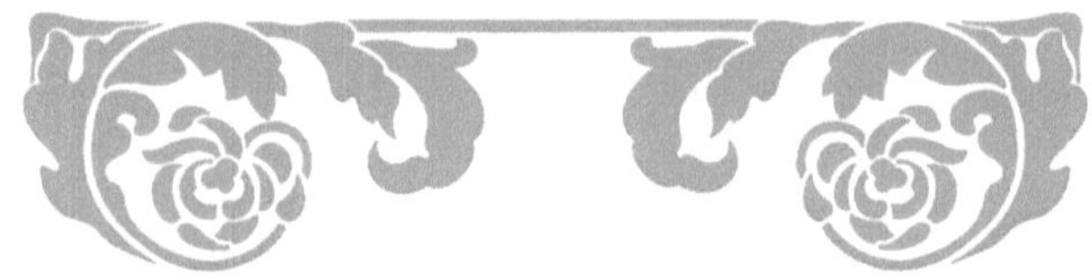

This book is for Zamion
who gave me the energy to get it done.

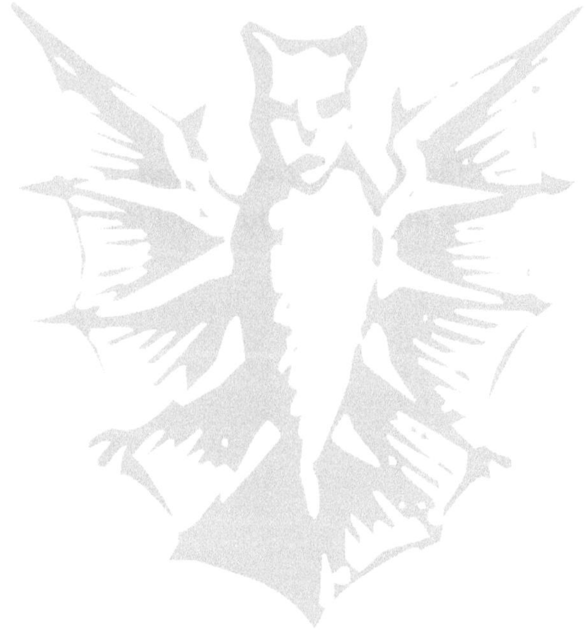

Introduction

Since I saw my first Hammerfilms, hosted by local television personality Superhost on lazy Saturday afternoons, I have been fascinated by those beautiful and terrible creatures that we call *vampires.*

Vampires have been such an interest of mine for so very long that I cannot properly recall what book or movie introduced us. I know that my mother and her sisters were all fans of the 1960s show, *Dark Shadows,* and they spoke enough about this when I was a child that I knew who Barnabas Collins was before the age of ten. But I was playing games that had vampires as a central theme with other children in the schoolyard as early as first grade. At what point that archetype took root in my head, I cannot say, but when that seed was dropped, those roots ran fast and deep.

An early reader, my grandmother had a peculiar sense of what constituted appropriate literature for a child. She regularly passed on her Stephen King novels whenever she was finished with them, and before my pre-teens I had steeped my imagination in the rich and vivid worlds of Bradbury, Hawthorne, Lovecraft, and Poe.

I very clearly recall seeking out a collection of Poe's short stories at the elementary school library. It was in the section for the fifth graders, and I was only in the third grade at the time. Technically I wasn't allowed to check the book out. Always a determined little thing, I grabbed the book anyway, marched up to the school librarian, opened it to a random page, and started reading (it was "The Cask of Amontillado" because I remember stumbling on that one word). After I proved that I could read what was in the book, she caved and let me check it out — with the warning that scary stories like that would keep me up all night.

They never did. The tales that others found frightening and macabre just fascinated me. All the stories of ghosts and goblins, witches — and of course, *vampires* — held me in thrall. While I understood that King and Bradbury and all the rest were writing fantasy, I also knew that there were stories that these creatures were based upon. Eventually I learned the names for such tales. Myths. Folklore. More than anything else, I wanted to get my hands on *that* literature. Always curious, always inquiring, I wanted to know if there was any truth to these beings, the boogeymen that frightened others but made me feel electric all over. Certainly, vampires stalked through the shadows on the television and at the movies, but were they — could they be — *real?*

Looking at that question years and pages of research later, I can appreciate the wide-eyed naïveté of that sentiment. These days, I always experience a sardonic inward chuckle when someone wonderingly asks me the same question. *Are vampires real?*

It all depends on what you mean by "vampire."

The creature Bram Stoker immortalized in fiction is something that is more than just words. This is evidenced by the very fact that Stoker's novel *Dracula* still sees publication at all. The book is imperfect. Stoker's style is stilted, stuffy, and contrived. And yet somehow, something lives on in this book that exceeds the limits of Stoker's marginal skill. That something is a potent archetype whose roots stretch to the depths of the human imagination and whose branches extend through nearly every aspect of our modern culture, from the board room to children's breakfast cereals.

Are vampires real? There are vampires aplenty to be found in myth and folklore. Nearly every culture the world over has some traditional creature that can be described as vampiric. These creatures drink blood, they travel abroad at night, and many of them walk the shadowy threshold between life and death. But some of them are also what we'd call witches, and others are faeries, and still others are werewolves. Are these folkloric monsters *vampires*? It all depends on where the reader or the researcher or the villager reporting the incident chooses to draw the line.

Are vampires real? The image of the vampire is so prevalent in literature and upon the stage that it has achieved a kind of reality to us. We experience characters like Angel and Lestat in a personal manner, and we see a little of ourselves in them. These characters are archetypes that have developed at least a psychological reality for some. They are real enough to serve as companions on a cold, lonely night, as the reader lays curled up in bed, the words marching steadily from page to page.

But are vampires real? You can go to certain clubs in Los Angeles or New York — even corn-fed, sleepy Ohio — and encounter people who are dressed as vampires. With their movie-monster contacts and their expertly crafted fangs, most are more convincing that Christopher Lee ever was. Some even feed upon energy. Some even drink blood.

But what is a vampire, really? The vampire is something that has grown beyond its folkloric roots. It is something that is different for different people: a symbol, an archetype, an aesthetic ideal, even a spiritual path. What is real about the vampire is the effect it has on people. They are romanced by it, thrilled, fascinated, and held in thrall. It is this internal, mythic reality that *Sacred Hunger* seeks to explore, revealing the vampire in all his many guises, through society, history, folklore, and myth.

The Secret World of Vampires

*This article was originally written for **Fate Magazine's** October 2004 issue. The article never went to print, but it seemed a shame to waste it. As it was intended to serve as an introduction to the vampire community for the readers of **Fate**, I felt it would make an excellent introductory article to this diverse collection.*

They gather each year around Halloween, haunting the streets of the French Quarter: black-clad people with strange, pale faces, tattooed and pierced, with wild, dyed hair. They walk through the city at night dressed as vampires. Some wear capes or other fashions from by-gone eras. Some sport contacts: cat's eyes; reptile eyes; eyes that are white or entirely black. And when they smile, pointed teeth protrude past their lips. The fangs are so subtle, so expertly done, it's hard to believe that they're fake.

As you take in the magic-filled nights of New Orleans, it's tempting to wonder: Is this all just part of the Halloween fun, or is there some truth hiding behind the masquerade?

It's easy to imagine New Orleans as the City of Vampires. Numerous spinners of the vampire yarn have chosen to set their stories here. Most famous among these is the novelist Anne Rice. Many of the tales in her *Vampire Chronicles* are set against the backdrop of a Gothic New Orleans. Her most famous creation, the vampire Lestat, maintains a fictional residence in the French Quarter, located on the very real Rampart Street. In a city that was once home to Marie Laveau, the Voodoo Queen, vampires seem hardly a stretch of the imagination.

Dead Man's Party

The French Quarter is renown for its wild, decadent parties. Most of the bars on Bourbon Street never really close. And while Mardi Gras celebrates the city's masked and beaded splendor, Halloween evokes a darker side. Endless Night, Dark Cotillion, Cirque du Nuit, and Dark Awakenings are only some of the Gothic-themed celebrations that attract the vampire-people in droves. And at least one of these gatherings openly explores the vampire as a being who is very, very real.

At Endless Night 2003, a much-feted book was debuted. Published by Vampyre Almanac, in conjunction with the Netherlands-based Aangel Publishing, the book was entitled simply *V*. A shiny black hard-backed tome, emblazoned with a blood-red, stylized "V", the book has the look of an ancient grimoire transplanted to the modern era. It claims to be a book written by vampires for vampires, "dedicated to the vampyre existence as a real experience."

This vampire existence is something that *V* labels "Strigoi Vii," derived from the Romanian term for "living vampires". Those who follow the path of Strigoi Vii believe themselves to be vampires -- not in the sense of undead immortals, but as beings who feed upon the life around them.

Many are "pranic" vampires, who take the vital life force of others in a process *V* terms "communion". Those familiar with metaphysics and the occult will recognize this as a type of psychic vampirism. However, what sets the vampires of the Strigoi Vii apart from typical psychic vampires is that they are fully aware of what they are. Further, based on the exercises and techniques outlined in Book II of *V,* they exercise complete volition in feeding.

V not only outlines methods for willfully taking the energy of others but it also outlines a code of ethics living vampires should follow when they feed. This code of conduct, recently featured on the "Suckers" episode of *CSI Vegas,* is called "The Black Veil". The name is possibly derived from the song "Long Black Veil" by the late Johnny Cash, but is also reminiscent of Nathaniel Hawthorne's story, "The Minister's Black Veil". Either source of inspiration brings to mind secrets that must be kept, and accordingly, the Black Veil stresses that its followers should use discretion when revealing their vampiric nature to those who might not understand.

However, the Black Veil goes further than simply encouraging secrecy. There is an honorable code of ethics lurking beneath the flowery language and sometimes melodramatic terms. For example, taking energy from someone without their permission is strongly discouraged. Instead, vampires are expected to feed from willing donors who are fully conversant with the techniques of energy exchange outlined in the second half of the book, the *Strigoi Vii Codex*. Excerpted from my own *Psychic Vampire Codex*, this instructional text shatters the typical image of a psychic vampire as someone who preys upon others without their consent. Instead, it suggests that those who are aware of their vampiric nature are subsequently empowered to make conscious, potentially ethical choices in how that nature is expressed.

Vampire Nation

As alluring as the atmosphere in the French Quarter may be to real-life vampires, New Orleans is by no means the only city where they can be

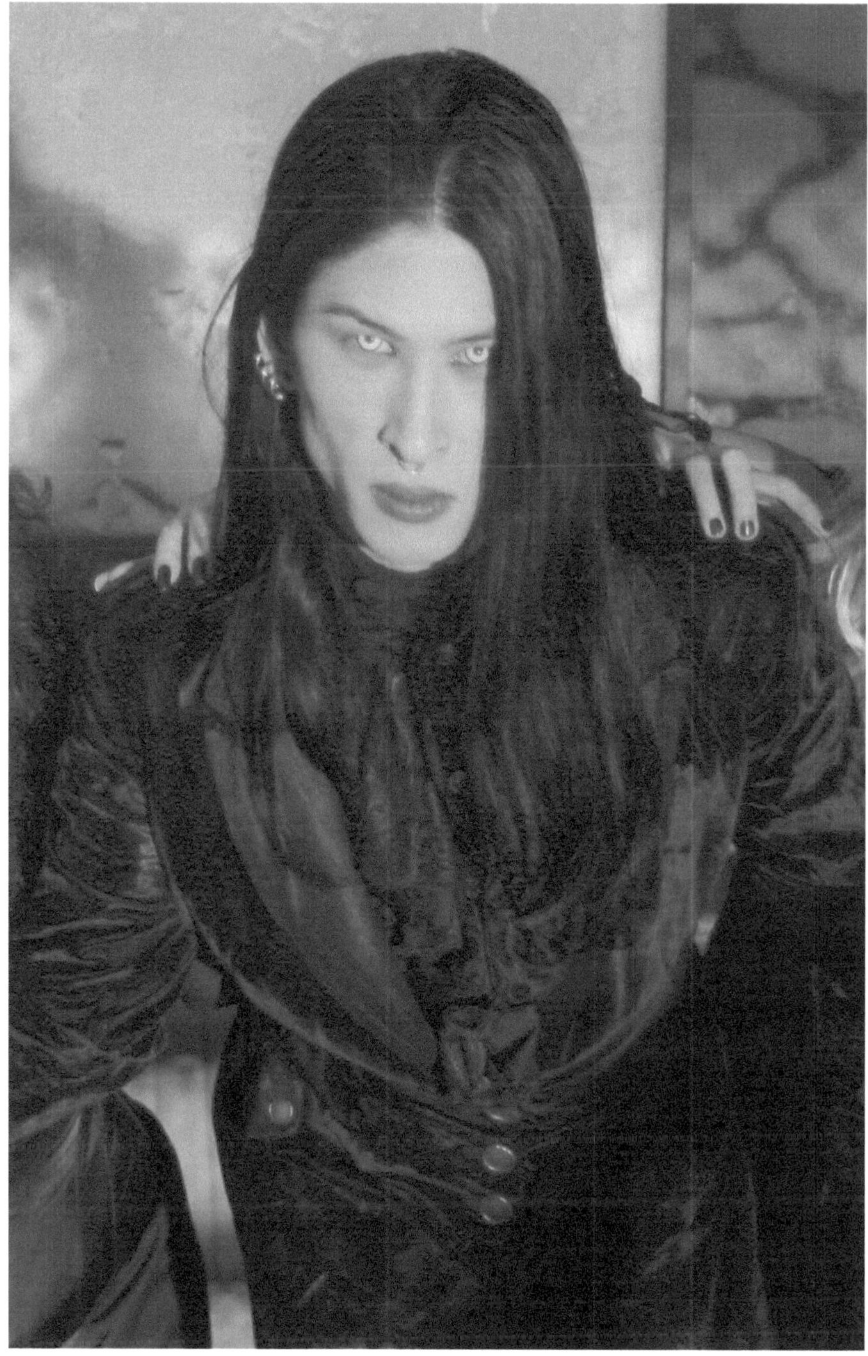

found. Groups of vampires, often termed "Houses", exist across the US, in Canada, most of Europe and even Japan. A brief search of the Internet reveals vampire Houses in such an amazing array, it's hard to believe they're for real. And yet members of some of these organizations are beginning to step forward and tell their tales.

Don Henrie is one of these. Featured as the practitioner of an alternative lifestyle on SciFi's *Mad, Mad House,* Don Henrie appears in high Gothic fashion, cupping a wineglass in one slender hand. White contacts give him an unnatural and yet strangely alluring gaze. Sharp, glossy fingernails cap each pale finger, and when he smiles it's impossible to miss his fangs. Don, a native of San Diego, is a former microelectric engineer. And in addition to his taste for Gothic fashion, Don Henrie also has a taste for human blood. As an expression of his vampire nature, Don Henrie regularly takes a small amount of blood from a willing donor who has been carefully screened for blood-borne diseases.

Although works like *V* encourage a greater focus on pranic energy, some members of the vampire community, like Don Henrie, get what they need through the medium of blood. Father Sebastian, the publisher of *V* and founder of the Sanguinarium, acknowledges that some members of the worldwide vampire community practice blood-drinking. But he strongly discourages this. "With all the diseases and other things to consider," Sebastian says, "blood's too much of a risk. Pranic feeding is the way to go." Offering safer, if less physical, methods is one of his reasons for publishing *V*.

Just as not all living vampires feed exclusively on energy, not all of them follow the path of the Strigoi Vii. Many of the Houses are independently run, and while they do adhere to some manner of ethical guidelines, the Black Veil is not perceived as universal law (despite *Mad, Mad House* typifying it as a "sacred document"). Diversity is a highly prized value in a community of people whose very nature sets them outside the bounds of normative society, and many of the vampires take pride in doing things their own way.

House of the Vampire

Each House has its own take on what vampirism really is, and each House often has its own unique symbol and theme. Some of the Houses are metaphysical groups that provide a place of instruction and acceptance for the vampires in their membership. Many others are just social groups, and they provide both a network and a meeting place for like-minded individuals to come together and share their experiences.

Among these Houses, which can range in membership from twelve to sixty people or more, even the word used to describe a living vampire may not be the same. Some call themselves sanguinarians. Others use *V*'s term of Strigoi Vii. Still others call themselves vampyres, using the more archaic spelling to distinguish themselves from the creatures of myth. Regardless the name, their basic belief remains the same: all are real, living people whose hunger for life inspires them to identify with the mythic archetype featured in fictional works such as *Dracula*, *Interview with the Vampire*, and *Buffy the Vampire Slayer*.

Some may dress the part, like the exotic Don Henrie, while others may look no more remarkable than the person standing next to you in line at the bank. Some may take life by feeding upon energy, while others may feed more traditionally upon human blood. They come from all races, all occupations, all ages. Yet all of them belong to the secret world of the vampire.

They may come out in force in New Orleans each Halloween, baring their fangs for the world to see. But when the holiday is over, they do not disappear in a puff of mist. Like everyone else, they board their planes and head for home. The contacts come out and they resume their routines: holding a job, having a family, paying the bills. Even *V*, with all its heady talk of pranic vampirism and energy exchange stresses that vampirism is just one part of a full and balanced existence. The real challenge it places before living vampires is to embrace what they are and integrate this into a normal life.

Romancing the Vampire

An early version of this article appeared in 1996 in ***Journal of the Dark*** *under the title "Evolution of an Archetype." Updated and revised, an expanded version of the article was produced for* ***Dark Realms*** *in 2004. Joseph Vargo of* ***Monolith Graphics*** *kindly contributed some of the closing material on the vampire in film.*

The vampire has come a long way since its beginnings in folklore. The compelling beings we encounter on the screen or in the works of Anne Rice, Chelsea Quinn Yarbro, Poppy Z. Brite, and Laurell K. Hamilton are elegant and seductive. Though monstrous in their hungers, there is an ineffable something that inspires many so-called "victims" to willingly open their veins. Yet in stark contrast, the vampires we encounter in the tales of Eastern Europe are little more than corpses. These foul and bestial monsters terrorize whole villages, filling their victims with horror and disgust.

Modern vampires have little in common with the *strigoi* and *nosferatu* of myth. Lestat, as the recent movie *Queen of the Damned* makes clear, is a sex symbol, plain and simple. And even Dracula is a compellingly erotic figure in the 1992 Francis Ford Coppola film. But how did the voluptuous Lestat or the elegant St. Germain evolve from the kind of creatures known to wallow in decaying coffins swimming with blood? How was a hideous creature of folklore transformed over the space of less than three hundred years into the demon lover so many desire?

Early Vampires

Prior to the 19th century, several treatises on vampires were written. These were primarily concerned with the identification and destruction of the undead and often included accounts of typical vampiric attacks, such as the classic case of Arnod Paole. Paole was a Serbian soldier from the early eighteenth century who often spoke of having been attacked early in his career by a vampire. When Paole later met his death in a fall from a haywagon, he himself returned as a vampire, sparking an epidemic of vampirism in his small village of Medvegia.

These early treatises read more like coroner's inquests than supernatural romances. Some were official reports of very serious investigations, while others were ecclesiastical works expounding the habits of a creature believed to be a very real threat to body and soul. It was not until 1748

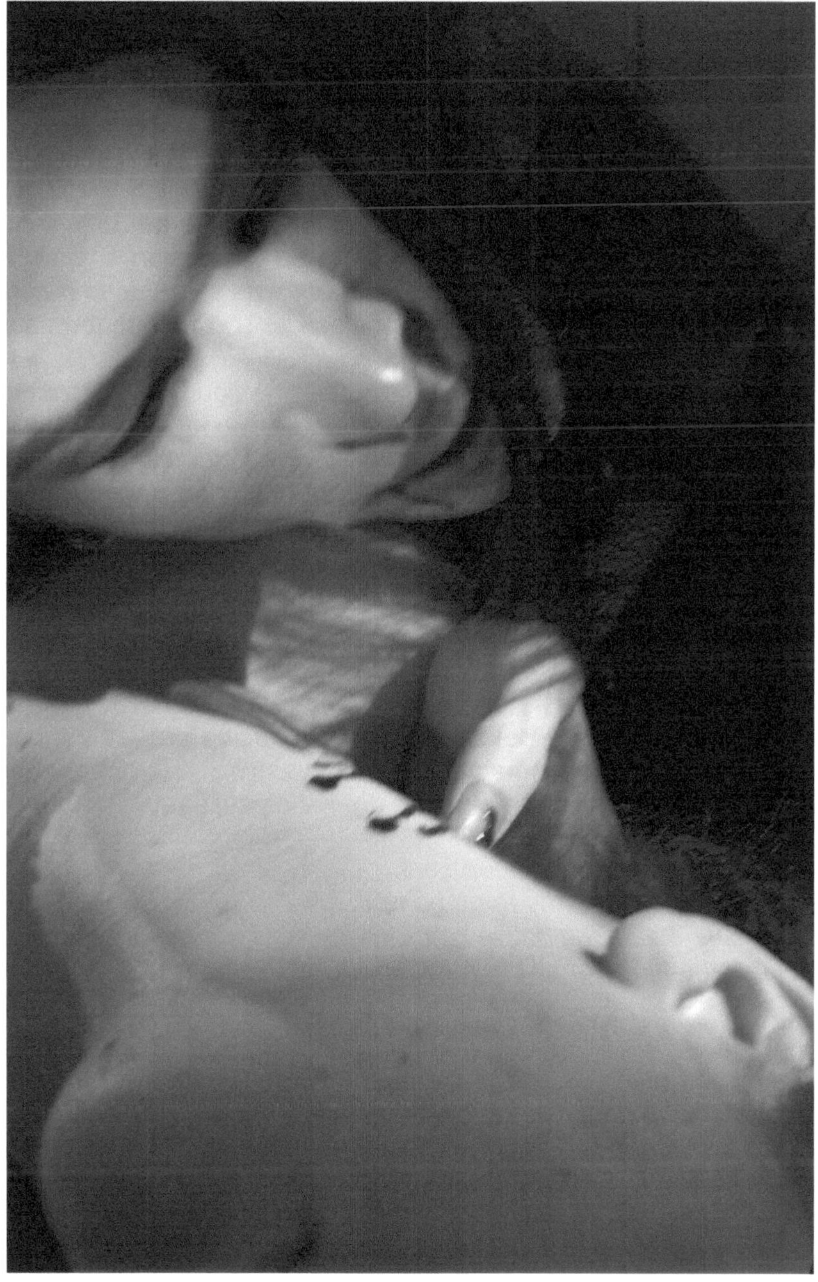

when Heinrich August Ossenfelder published his poem, "Der Vampir" did the figure of the vampire appear in a literary work.

Later, near the end of the century, both Goethe and Samuel Taylor Coleridge produced works which featured vampiric entities. The more interesting of these two is Coleridge's long poem, "Christabel." This work marks a milestone in vampire literature because the villainess in the poem, Geraldine, is a lesbian as well as a vampire.

This may seem a side issue, but actually it is a very telling detail of the literary vampire's developing nature. In the unenlightened 18th century, a homosexual lifestyle was seen as worse than a perversion; it was against nature and against God. In fact, homosexuality was about as unnatural and abhorrent in the eyes of the common populace as a corpse that rose nightly from its grave to drink the blood of the living.

What Coleridge succeeds in doing through the figure of Geraldine is for the first time overtly to couple sexual taboos with vampirism. The literary vampire, as it developed in the nineteenth century, serves most often as a symbol for the darker regions of human nature, those parts of ourselves which are never exposed to the light of day. Thus the vampire becomes the other, the forbidden, the outcast; ultimately, it is everything within ourselves which we at once revile and desire.

Byron, Lord of Vampires

After Coleridge, the next vampire writer of note is Lord Byron, a man who seemed to devote his life to exploring and embracing precisely those dark regions of human nature inhabited by the vampire. Byron produced a poem, "The Giaour," which gives us the dramatic passage:

"But first, on earth, as vampire sent,
Thy corpse shall from thy tomb be rent,
And ghastly, haunt thy native place,
And suck the blood of all thy race."

Byron, lines 755-758

However, as much as Byron clearly had a fascination for the figure of the vampire, his extant works on the subject would probably not have earned him a place in the canon of vampire literature. That distinction, instead, was achieved through a work written *about* Lord Byron entitled *The Vampyre.*

The Vampyre is the first full-length fictional work of vampire literature to appear in the English language. Authored by John William Polidori, *The Vampyre* bases its main character, Lord Ruthven, upon the darkly romantic

Lord Byron. The character of Lord Ruthven was actually originated by another one of Byron's scorned lovers, Lady Caroline Lamb, who sought revenge on Byron by creating a perverse caricature of him in her gothic novel, *Glenarvon*.

Polidori, a brilliant if erratic man prone to fits of melancholy, spent several months as Byron's personal physician. Completely infatuated with Byron, Polidori's advances were nevertheless met with the cruelest scorn. As a kind of revenge, Polidori demonized Byron through the main character of *The Vampyre*.

Erroneously published under Byron's name in 1819 and allegedly based upon a fragmentary story of his design (some say Polidori did this intentionally to boost sales), *The Vampyre* features the courtly and seductive Lord Ruthven whose appearance, mannerisms, and personality are a not very subtle caricature of Lord Byron himself. The fundamental difference seems to be the fact that Ruthven preys only upon virgins; Byron himself was not quite that particular.

Throughout the novel, Polidori tries to demonstrate how base and wicked Ruthven is, but his own ambivalent desires toward Byron make the character far more complex than any mere caricature of a spurning lover. This is arguably the first tale where we begin to see the figure of the vampire openly presented as both alluring and repulsive, noble yet bestial. With Ruthven, Polidori explores the extremes of human nature through the exploration of an inhuman beast. This was a fundamental turning point in the literary history of the vampire.

A Most Seductive Beast

Polidori's Ruthven is the first example of the seductive vampire we know today. Gone is the sepulchral paraphernalia and charnel-house breath of the folklore-inspired vampires. Ruthven, instead, is a modern 19th century gentleman, commanding, charismatic, eloquent, and impeccably dressed. All these expressions of a noble and civilized nature are thinly painted over Ruthven's true and hideous nature, but in some respects, this only makes him that much more alluring.

Despite his intrinsic evil, Ruthven is still something of a sympathetic character. He is depicted clearly as the outsider, a man whose "leaden gaze" cannot pierce to the soul of another but must remain weighing morosely against the barrier of the skin. He manipulates the narrator, Aubrey, and ultimately causes his ruin, yet he also earns Aubrey's love and admiration.

In an oblique reflection of "Christabel," Aubrey's relationship with Ruthven is driven by an underlying yet unspoken homoeroticism. Certainly there is something in Ruthven which Aubrey's sister finds to love as well, yet Ruthven can only reciprocate by destroying her, too.

Despite Polidori's attempts to malign Byron through his vampire character, Ruthven develops into an essentially tragic figure, much like the poet actually was. Ruthven's very nature denies him intimacy; he is devoured from within by an overwhelming sense of isolation, yet he can only devour those who come close to him in a desperate attempt to fill the void. The kind of dark pathos evoked by Ruthven has come to define the psychologically complex and sexually alluring vampire of today.

Little Girl Vamp

The dark pathos of the vampire is further drawn upon by Joseph Sheridan LeFanu in his 1872 tale, "Carmilla." Created at the height of the Victorian era, "Carmilla" is fueled by a subtle, driving sexuality. Without lifting a petticoat, LeFanu's title character pursues her prey with a tortured zeal, always choosing to feed upon young women close to her own apparent age.

The homoeroticism of this vampire tale is far more overt than even that of *The Vampyre* and it is infinitely more disturbing. Victorian audiences undoubtedly found the story scandalous, but even many modern readers still find themselves uncomfortable with the psychodynamics of the tale. In his classic work on the vampire, Basil Copper notably mistakes the narrator and heroine of the tale for a young boy; apparently he was unable even in the 70s to conceive of such sexually charged scenes occurring between two young girls.

Despite her unnatural appetites, there are points throughout the story where Carmilla seems more a victim than her innocent prey. She has clearly not chosen to be what she is and she vacillates between being a heartless, calculating monster and a mournful, frightened girl.

Count Dracula

The era of the Romantic vampire peaked in 1897 when an obscure Irishman published an epistolary novel whose title character was loosely based upon an ancient Transylvanian ruler, Vlad Tepes. Bram Stoker's creation has become synonymous with the vampire, and there are few people in the modern world who would fail to recognize the name, Dracula. Stoker's novel also finished the work that Polidori began, elaborating on the old folklore and establishing characteristics which we still recognize today as hallmarks of the undead. In this modern era, everyone knows that vampires cast no reflection, can turn into wolves or bats, and are repelled by the cross. Yet all of these were inventions of Stoker, and they have no solid basis in any of the earlier folklore.

Bram Stoker's tale of the reclusive Transylvanian count who leaves his castle domain in search of love is a bittersweet balance of unearthly terror and poignant romance, and perhaps no single author has been more responsible for the vampire's transition from the loathsome creature of folklore to the seductive and suave character that we know today.

Bela Lugosi's elegant portrayal of the charismatic Count Dracula in the acclaimed theatrical production of Stoker's novel won him the starring role in the classic 1931 film version of *Dracula*. Directed by Todd Browning, this motion picture was a major turning point in the way the vampire would come to be perceived in the 20th century. Lugosi's enchanting European accent and hypnotic stare lent a romantic voice and face to this bloodthirsty creature of the night.

In the late 1970s, Frank Langella took the vampire myth to new erotic heights with his passionate portrayals of Dracula on stage and screen. Gary Oldman's brilliant performance in the 1992 Francis Ford Coppola production beautifully illustrated both sides of this complex character, portraying the horrific and the romantic faces of Dracula with equal finesse. In this visually stunning film, Dracula was depicted in the guises of beast, demon, and withered ghoul, and yet he was perceived as a sympathetic and romantic character who had sacrificed his mortal soul for love.

EVOLUTION

The vampire's evolution from the sinister abominations of folklore and myth to the seductive and irresistible anti-hero of modern fiction and film is a complex and fascinating study. Though this transition is the result of more than two hundred and fifty years of popular literature, it stands as a testament to the writers who each gave a little of their own life and soul to the figure of the vampire.

Today, the word "vampire" is listed in Roget's International Thesaurus as a synonym for *fiend* and *monster* as well as *tempter* and *seducer.* With so complex a face, it is small wonder that the vampire continues to fascinate and inspire us in fiction, film, and private dreams.

Monster-Hunting in Romania

In my days at John Carroll University, there were two books at Grasselli library that I poured over again and again. One was collection of photographs of London's Highgate Cemetery. The other was ***The Were-Wolf and Vampire in Romania*** *by Harry A. Senn. Senn's treatise on cultural anthropology was one of best resources I had ever found on vampire folklore. The book provided material for a number of short pieces in* ***The Midnight Sun****, most notably one that addressed the Romanian idea of living vampires. When the vampire network known as the Sanguinarium transformed itself into the OSV, the term it adopted to indicate modern, living vampires was derived from the material covered in this article. That early, influential piece forms the kernel of what appears below.*

Between the years of 1976 to 1979, Harry A. Senn traveled to Romania in search of monsters. Seeking evidence of werewolves, vampires, and witches, Senn's travels took him through isolated villages where the way of life had changed very little since the time that a dictator named Vlad Tepes had ruled over a Transylvanian kingdom called Wallachia.

The historic Dracula had nothing to fear from this self-appointed monster-hunter, however. Senn was no modern-day Van Helsing. A folklorist working on a scholarly dissertation, Senn was not seeking his vampires and other monsters in the depths of the Transylvanian woods, but in the living oral traditions of the people residing there. Even so, what Senn discovered during his Transylvanian excursion may still prove shocking to the rest of the modern world. The vampire — or at least the belief in such a being — was alive and well in 20th century Romania.

Of the Romanian villagers interviewed by Senn, many reported a belief in werewolves, witches, and vampires. The folktales that Senn gathered about these otherworldly creatures had changed very little since the centuries during which corpses were regularly exhumed and mutilated due to the suspicion that they were in fact undead.

Perhaps one of the first points that stands out in Senn's study is that the lines between these three traditional monsters are not as distinct in folklore as they have become in our modern literary tradition. Indeed, in our modern culture, the witch is hardly even seen as a monster anymore, having shed her role as a folkloric boogeyman who casts harmful spells upon her neighbors and instead been reclaimed as a positive and empowering image by those who follow the Wiccan and neo-Pagan religion.

In movies like *Underworld*, vampires and werewolves are often depicted as being at odds with one another. And yet, when we dig past the pop culture façade to the very source of words like "vampire," the Eastern European homelands of these myths yield some startling facts. Several of the words used to identify vampires were originally used in reference to werewolves. This is true of the Russian *volkodlak*, which is composed of *volk,* or "wolf," and *dlak,* meaning "hair." The Romanian *pricolici*, which is identified by Raymond T. McNally in his biography of Dracula as an alternate word for "vampire," can be broken down into *irpu* and *liciu.* These mean "turned into" and "wolf," respectively. The Greek *vyrkolakas* also shares this original meaning of "wolf-skinned" or "wolf-haired."

Shape-Shifting Monsters

In folklore around the world, vampires, witches, and werewolves all share the ability to transform into animals. Frequently, this bestial transmogrification involves wolves, but sometimes an individual transforms into another predatory or night-dwelling creature. Folktales from the ancient Middle East to the steppes of Russia tell of people who can assume the form of bats, owls, hyenas, and even great cats in order to go abroad at night and create mischief. In Africa, this is a common ability ascribed to witches, who are also purported to drink human blood.

Senn's study shows us that only in our popular imagination are the lines of demarcation between vampires, werewolves, and witches absolutely distinct. Practically every child in America could explain that vampires sleep in coffins because they are "undead." And yet, the Romanian villagers interviewed for Senn's book did not even universally identify vampires as *dead.* According to the 1970s research, there are, in fact, *living* vampires. These are individuals, born with some stain, defect, or curse, who exhibit vampiric qualities throughout their lives.

The main term that Senn recognizes as indicative of a vampire is the Romanian *strigoi mort.* He describes these as the "walking dead," beings who return from the grave to work mischief. They suck blood, and sometimes cause living people to sicken and die, but more frequently they are noted among the Romanians for sucking milk. On the other side of the coin is the *strigoi vii,* the living vampire, sometimes also referred to as *moroi* or *moroaica.*

Living vampires share most, if not all, of the powers attributed to their undead kin. In addition to stealing the vitality of others, willfully or unconsciously, the living vampires are also credited as having the evil eye. While some are reputed to suck the blood of infants, their life-stealing powers are by no means limited to blood. In fact, they are more often depicted as using their powers to take milk from cattle or to sap the vitality from fields of grain.

The Vampiric Witch

All of these qualities will be familiar to anyone conversant with those powers attributed to witches during the European Witchcraze. The nefarious 15th century witch-finding tome, *The Malleus Maleficarum* ("Hammer of Witches"), lists almost precisely the same abilities under spells believed to be cast through witchcraft.

Witches blight fields, make cattle go barren, cause their udders to dry up, and with a word or a look can cause an unfortunate neighbor to sicken and waste away. Most witches were also attributed with the ability to assume the form of a dog or cat in order to carry out their mischief anonymously. In the documents of the witch-hunts, some witches were blamed for plagues that decimated entire villages, and, as observed by Paul Barber in his classic, *Vampires, Burial, and Death,* vampires were often attributed with having done the same.

In Italy, one of the words for a witch is *strega.* This word was handed down from Roman times and derived from *strix,* a kind of diabolical screech owl believed to drink human blood. The Romanian *strigoi* is derived from the same root. More properly translated, it simply means "witch." A *strigoi mort* is simply a dead — or undead — witch, while the *strigoi vii* is a living witch. *Strigoi* are believed to be marked from birth. Romanians believe that a child born with a little tail, or a caul, or, rarer still, twinned pupils, will grow up to become a *strigoi vii,* while after their death, they are foredoomed to return as a *strigoi mort.*

In either of these cases, the source of the "curse" is an incomplete transition from one world to the next. With the undead, this is obvious. They are restless spirits, unwilling or unable to cross completely from one world to the next. Caught in a state between the living and the dead, they exist outside of nature, and therefore exist beyond the bounds of natural laws. Bereft of a life of their own to sustain them, they must naturally seek out the life force contained in blood or milk or even fertile fields.

The child born with a caul or tail likewise has made an incomplete transition from one world to the next. The otherworld clings to this child, and the caul or tail is physical proof that the child has retained qualities that are more than human. This lingering connection to something that exists outside of ordinary nature manifests as magical power. Having been caught in between the living and the dead all his or her life, it only makes sense that an individual thus marked will continue to linger in a liminal state after physical death.

Twice-Born vs. Undead

All of these qualities of magic, undeath, and shape-shifting come together in another Eastern European figure that also has echoes in folk traditions around the world. Deep in the Tungus, Siberian region of Russia, and having cognate traditions among the primary peoples of every continent, there is a being who is believed to exist outside of the normal boundaries of life and death. Such a being is believed to have started off as a normal member of the village or tribe. However, after a crisis of extreme illness, characterized by visionary states and a brush with death, that individual comes back *changed.* Gifted with the ability to see in complete darkness, converse with spirits, transform into animals, and fly through the heavens as a spirit himself, this changed individual is known as a *shaman.*

Although popularized in the Western imagination as a strictly Native American tradition, shamanism is a phenomenon that is worldwide. Shamans were specialized healers who served a specific function for their communities as intermediaries between the world of the living and the world of the dead. Shamans were seen as being both gifted and cursed by their unique abilities. Known as "the wounded healer," the shaman could wield power over life and death because he himself had died and yet survived. Death clung to him still, and it was only through the mastery of his powers that he maintained the ability to heal himself and, by extension, others.

The shamanic initiation, which always involved an illness that brought the shaman to the very brink of death, was believed to quite literally kill him. Holger Kalweit, in *Dreamtime and Inner Space,* tells of shamans who were so close to death that their families had begun funeral proceedings for them, only to have the "corpse" wake up and begin speaking at the funeral. One lucky shaman, who had been placed upon his funeral pyre, returned from the trance state of shamanic initiation just as the first flames were beginning to rise.

The crisis illness of shamanic initiation earned the shaman his title of "twice-born," a term that is distinctly similar in meaning to the more infamous "undead." That a shaman, like the *strigoi* recorded in Senn's work, made an incomplete transition from one world to the next is not in dispute. The power of the shaman arises from his very status as a liminal being, and it is this liminality that allows him to travel freely across the barriers that separate man from animal, the living from the dead. The question that arises, once a comparison has been made between the beneficial shaman and the predatory vampire, is: *what really makes them distinct?*

Against Man or Nature

Witches, among the Romanian villagers, are not seen as automatically evil beings. To be a *strigoi pe bani* is to be a "witch for money," which is to say that one has an uncanny knack for turning a profit. Similar expressions describe how people can be witches for music and other constructive work. Thus, *strigoi* are tolerated when their powers are used for the good of the community. Even some of the more inimical creatures described in Senn's work, like the *pricolici,* are believed to have a functional role within the community when they are not in the throes of their lycanthropic curse.

This attitude of social versus anti-social behavior is not limited purely to vampires and *strigoi.* Mircea Eliade tells us of so-called "black shamans" who use their powers to attack and even kill their enemies. Such shamans do not have a welcome place within society because they work against its rules. While the power of a shaman or other magickal being is derived from his existence beyond of the natural order, that existence is only acceptable when it is used to help maintain that natural order for others.

This theme is best illustrated by the Slovenian tradition of the *kudlak* and *kresnik,* as recounted by Matthew Bunson. These are both powerful shape-shifters, shaman-like magicians who are believed to be wrapped in an eternal struggle. The *kudlak* attempts continuously to destroy the community, while the *kresnik* fights to protect it.

Senn elaborates on this dichotomous pair by describing the protective *kresnik* at once as a "sun-hero" but also pointing out that he is traditionally undead. The *kudlak,* presumably a living person, is therefore less of a liminal creature, and, in this sense, is less inherently "against nature" than something that is undead. Even so, it is the *kudlak,* and not the *kresnik* that is seen as the monster in this mythic struggle.

The defining factor of a monster, then, is not his otherworldly nature but what he chooses to use that nature for. Vampires cross the line between life and death, and then proceed to use the powers this grants them to prey upon others. The shaman crosses that line and returns to the community, using his otherworldly powers in service to the natural world. *Strigoi,* vampire, shaman, or witch, it is the choice to work for more than the self that separates the heroes from their monstrous twins.

A Sacred Hunger

*Originally published on **disinfo.com**, this article was one of a series done on the vampire Don Henrie and his performance on **Mad, Mad House**. The article actually started life as a Live Journal entry which fans requested that I enlarge upon and expand. It was through this and related articles that I came to correspond directly with Don who ultimately became a close friend.*

In the spring of 2004, the SciFi network aired a reality TV show entitled, *Mad, Mad House*. The concept behind this innovative venture was to select "average joes" and have them all live in a mansion with representatives of several exceptionally alternative lifestyles and/or fringe beliefs. The alternative lifestylers, or "alts", as they were called on the show, were given free reign of the mansion, and it was their responsibility to design and judge various elimination-style competitions that challenged the average joes' acceptance of their unusual beliefs, practices, and lifestyles.

One of the "alts" was San Diego native Don Henrie. Half-Welsh and half-Japanese, Don Henrie is a former microelectric engineer. He is also a practicing vampire. In addition to his vampirism, which includes the ingestion of both vital energy (*chi*) and human blood, Don Henrie is also highly psychic and practices spiritual alchemy and astral projection.

As a member of the vampire community, I took an interest both in the show and in Don Henrie. My main concern was seeing how Don and SciFi chose to portray his vampirism. During the course of the show, each "alt" had one show where he or she got to be the focus of things. For this show, that "alt" had to put together a ritual or some sort that showcased his or her particular alternative practices and beliefs.

Episode 6 was the one dedicated to Don Henrie, and therefore to vampirism. And though I had some inside knowledge of what was to transpire for this episode, I still watched it avidly to see how things had been edited. During his session, Don demonstrated a technique of psychic vampirism where, by the laying on of hands, he withdrew enough vital energy from a volunteer to cause that person (Noel, from among the "average joes") to collapse and pass out. After his demonstration on Noel, Don then brought in his girlfriend and donor, Gina, and he demonstrated a far more controversial aspect of his vampirism: the drinking of human blood.

While it was clear some of this demonstration had been edited to play

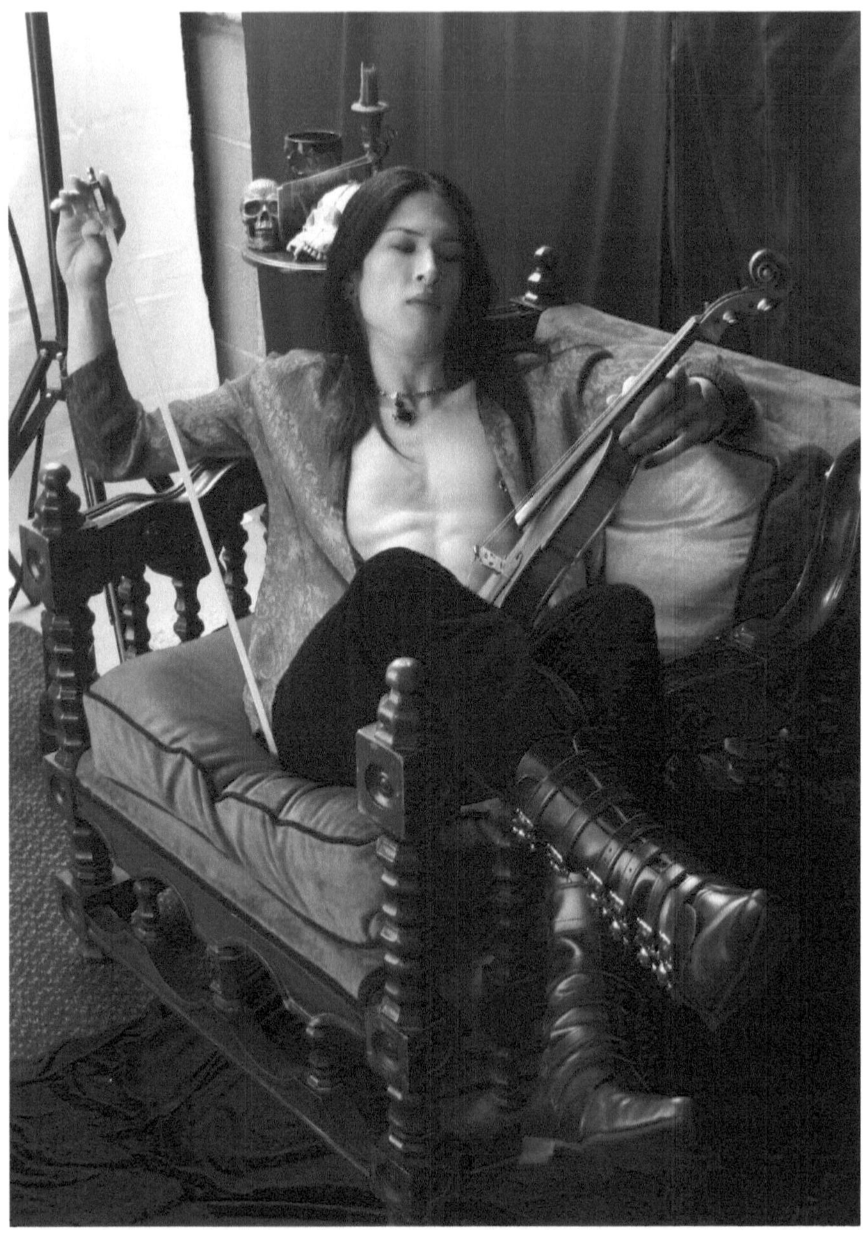

up on its sensational aspects, on the whole, I felt the demonstration was well done. Certainly, there were plenty of ways it could have been done worse. And the other people participating in the *Mad, Mad House*, with a few notable exceptions, generally reacted in an adult and open-minded fashion to Don's sharing of his most intimate practices.

After the episode aired, I of course kept an eye on the public's reaction to see how the average viewer felt about seeing a real, live vampire feed.

Now, I've always assumed that people outside our community would have the hardest time believing in the psychic aspect of vampirism. And yet, as I watched peoples' reactions to Don Henrie's display of sanguine vampirism on episode 6 of *Mad, Mad House*, I got something of a surprise. Although Don had attempted to explain the subtler aspects of what he was doing, people still kept trying to force his vampiric practices into a materialist paradigm. Outside the notion of eating or drinking something for physical sustenance or medical support, the vast majority of viewers just couldn't grasp it.

Although I myself am not a blood-drinker, I do understand what Don and other sanguine vampires get out of blood. The bottom line is that vampirism of any sort will make not sense if one tries to perceive it in a purely materialist light. A vampire's sanguine hunger cannot be rationalized through medical terms. It is pointless to try to argue that drinking blood cannot cure anemia and has no real nutritional value. Modern vampires are not self-medicating by drinking blood. They do not expect to get any *physical* sustenance from the blood whatsoever. The blood is merely a focus. It is the physical expression of the life force which courses subtly through all beings.

If blood as a more than physical substance still seems confusing, one has only to refer to the books of Deuteronomy and Leviticus and review the Kosher laws to see otherwise. The Bible says "The Blood is the Life." What is stated in the rest of the related passages is that the blood contains the *ruach* of an animal. *Ruach* is the Hebrew equivalent of *chi*, another word that can be translated as breath/life/spirit. So the Lord God forbids his people from eating the blood of an animal because the blood is a carrier for that animal's life-force, its spirit -- and in their views that life/spirit properly belongs only to God, from whom it originated.

Significantly, in the extra-Biblical text *The Book of Enoch*, one of the sins committed by the Nephilim (children of the angels who came down and intermarried with the daughters of men in the pre-Flood world) was the drinking of blood. This was seen as an abomination because the blood was sacred. The blood carried the life and the spirit, and the bastard sons of the angels were drinking what the Lord God had reserved only for Himself. It was because the angel-born Nephilim were committing the sin of stealing what God had reserved for himself, in addition to teaching humanity the arts of magick, of cosmetics, and of warfare, that the angels still loyal to the Lord urged him to punish both the Nephilim and humanity with the Flood.

Now, this is not to say that modern vampires are necessarily connected to the Nephilim. Rather, I'm pointing these stories out to show that at the roots of both Christianity and Judaism, there is a precedent for blood being more than just a physical substance. If you reduce it to platelets, hemoglobin, and plasma, you miss the point.

Cultures the world over have attributed blood with a sacred power, and several ancient peoples drank the blood of their slain enemies in a ritual exchange intended to help them gain those enemies' power through the magick of their blood. Blood was considered a worthy sacrifice even by the ancient Jews because it held power -- the physical substance was a vehicle for the real sacrifice, which was life force.

It is this sacred aspect of blood that Don Henrie and other blood-drinking vampires are tapping into. This is the mystical portion of Don's lifestyle that renders it a belief system on an equal level with witchcraft and Voudun -- hence his inclusion on *Mad, Mad House* to begin with. Don is not just dressing up for a fashion statement and he's not just drinking blood to sate a fetish. There is a very real phenomenon driving Don that may be obscured for some people by his love for the Gothic aesthetic and flamboyant fashion.

The vampire Don takes life -- indirectly through the medium of blood or directly in the form of energy/chi -- because it enriches and empowers him. He thirsts for that life because there is a side to his everyday experience of the world that is not just physical but metaphysical -- and the life energy of blood strengthens and nourishes his spiritual self just as his physical body is nourished and strengthened with more traditional fare.

Coming Out of the Coffin

This is one of the older articles in this collection. Originally written in 1999 for my House Kheperu website, it has been reprinted, with minor changes, on a variety of other vampire-related sites, including Sphynxcat's Real Vampires page, Sanguinarius.org, and the old Sanguinarium site. It offers a great deal of insight into why I do what I do, and why I feel it's important that others speak out about their vampirism as well.

When I started publishing articles on psychic vampirism in magazines and on the Web many years ago, I took a risk that few people were willing to do: with all my writings and interviews, I used my real name. Don't get me wrong – writing so openly about vampirism was not a comfortable thing, especially not at first. I knew I was sticking my neck out and could expect censure from friends, family members, and even strangers on the street. More than that, I knew that there were whole aspects of my future that such a public outing of myself made null and void.

First and foremost, I was giving up any chance I might have at any "normal" career in the mainstream world. As a National Merit Scholar and *magna cum laude* graduate of a prestigious private university, this was no small thing. With my scholastic credentials and my writing skills, I think it's fair to say that I was brimming with potential. And yet at the juncture of my emergence into the hallowed halls of academia, I found that it was more important to me to apply all that talent, creativity, and potential toward helping people understand vampires and vampirism. Certainly I could have gone on to a prestigious career as a professor at some time-honored college or university – but for me, that life would have been personally empty. Even looking down that path now, knowing what I let slip away, I do not regret the choice I made to write about something so reviled and so obscure.

For me, this is all about basic human rights, and I often turn to the human rights movement when I need inspiration. Fifty years ago, it was a terrible thing to be gay. As the homosexual marriage debate continues to divide whole countries in two, I think it's fair to say that it's still pretty tough to be gay, but forward motion has been made. Gay marriage is a reality in several areas of the world, and in the United States, many States are adopting partner benefits and laws that prevent workplaces from discriminating against employees based on their sexual orientation. Fifty years ago, however, homosexuality was still considered not only an aberration against God and nature, but it was also one of many "mental illnesses" treated with electroshock therapy.

Compare that to vampirism today. Most people, if you tell them that you're a vampire, are going to assume that you're crazy. I can bet dollars to donuts that if you tell your doctor or therapist about your vampirism, they will treat you for some mental illness. If, on some odd chance, the person you out yourself to *doesn't* assume that you're a sadly deluded psychopath, they are still highly likely to react to you with fear and suspicion. Pagans, Wiccans, New Agers, and other occultists who actually believe in the existence of psychic vampires almost universally despise them. Vampirism is truly the homosexuality of the magickal world: most "normal" magickal workers view it as an aberration, and I've actually heard Wiccans describe the act of vampirism as an unnatural act against the Goddess.

Consider the following, taken from a 1996 publication by Konstantinos called *Vampires: the Occult Truth*. The chapter is devoted to "Intentional Psychic vampires" and begins with these words:

> *These are the darkest creatures ... intentional psychic vampires can become monsters in every sense of the word ... the psychic vampires dealt with here freely choose to become what they are.*

Konstantinos does not have a very high opinion of us. His book, which professes to be the first which contains a tried and true method of protecting oneself from psychic vampire attacks, is one of the only books out on the market which addresses vampirism as a real occult phenomenon. This is a sad fact, because although Konstantinos has some legitimate insight into the nature and function of psychic vampirism, his view of the phenomenon is terribly one-sided. Throughout the text, vampires are presented as nothing but a threat to magickal workers and other innocent people. He consistently uses negative language to describe vampires and the act of vampirism, and his overall message is that vampires are out there and intent upon victimizing anyone they can. To return to the gay analogy, Konstantinos winds up sounding a lot like those religious fanatics who denounce homosexuality as the greatest corruption of our age and who feel that the very presence of a homosexual in a community is a threat to every straight person in that community. Vampirism, in Konstantinos's mind, is an insidious evil that no one is safe from -- unless, of course, they use his technique of psychic protection.

If Konstantinos were an isolated case, his book would hardly upset me as much as it does. And yet wherever I go in the Pagan and Wiccan com-

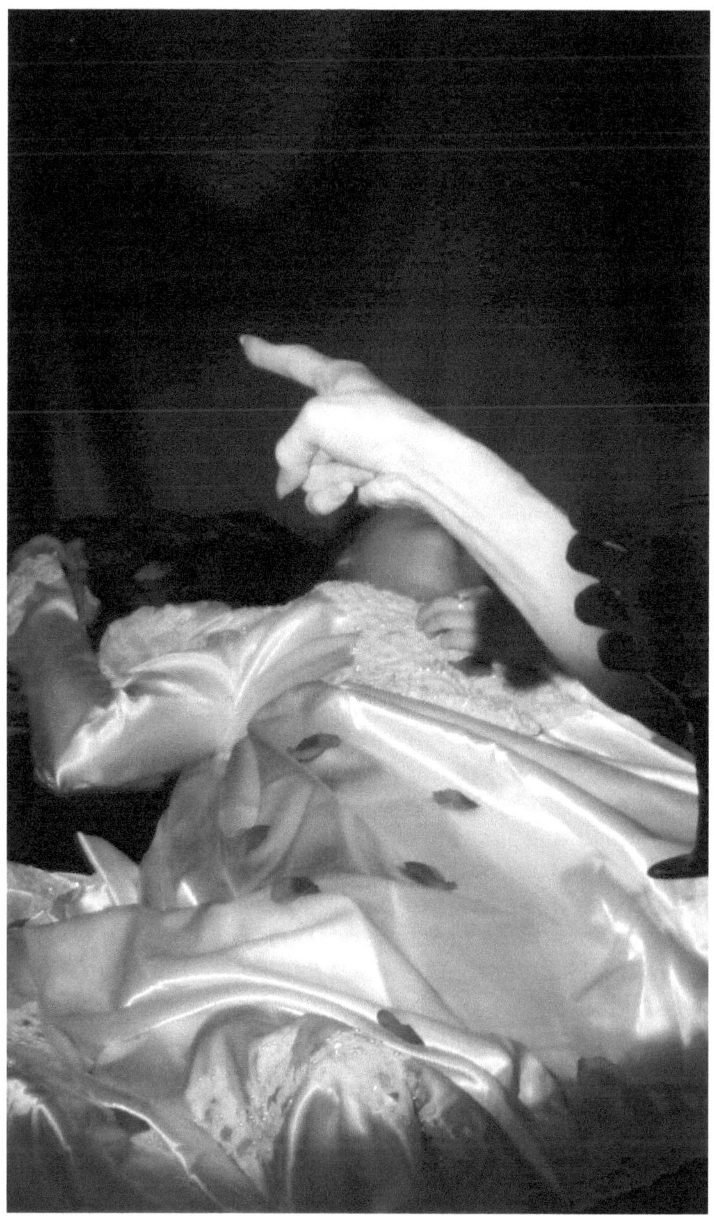

munity, I encounter sentiments similar to his. A few years ago, there was a convention in Seattle called Northwest Con that featured among its lectures a panel devoted to the issue of vampires. A friend of mine attended the panel discussion, eager to hear other peoples' opinions on the phenomenon. Those leading the panel claimed to hold positions of importance and respect within the local Pagan and Wiccan community. And to my friend's disappointment, all they had to offer were the same misconceptions and alarmist beliefs about vampires. According to the panel speakers, vampires were everywhere, and good Pagans and magickal workers had to be prepared to protect themselves from the evil of vampiric attack.

At best, energy workers view vampires as sick and in need of healing. A very close friend of mine from Modesto, California, is an excellent example of this. He is a first generation American, his family having come from China. His family runs a chi-healing institute and shrine in Modesto. My friend, whom we'll call Casey, was instructed in his particular form of chi-healing by his father. Casey is very gifted at this technique, and he is always willing to share his gifts to help friends, acquaintances, and even perfect strangers.

I met Casey at a convention in 1995 and he immediately took an interest in me. Apparently, the technique he used for diagnosing a person's wellness made me stand out in his eyes. He wasn't certain what was wrong with me as he had never encountered anything quite like it before, but he was too curious not to pursue me in order to figure out what was up. Once we had established that what he was seeing in me wasn't something that was "broken," we had a long conversation about our beliefs and practices and compared the way in which we both perceived and manipulated energy. He accepted what I was without judgment, although he was surprised to have encountered a legitimate one. He had, to his knowledge, never run into a real vampire before, although now that he knew what to look for, he was curious to check out a few people he knew back home.

We exchanged energy, mostly because he wanted to see just how much I could take. His technique, much like Reiki, taps him into a universal and virtually unlimited flow of energy. After several hours of this experiment, we decided to call it a draw, although he was amazed at my capacity to devour energy as much as I was amazed at his capacity to produce a seemingly endless supply.

Casey offered several times to try and help me, although he was certain it was beyond his capacity to heal what he perceived to be a great big hole in my energy body right around the Hara or Navel Chakra. In the years that followed, Casey and I have maintained contact and swapped techniques and experiences. He has been trying to perfect a technique which might restore what he considers a defect in my energy body and has consulted some teachers on the possibility of constructing a replacement Hara. He admits the technique is a long-shot, but for him it's a fascinating puzzle to be solved. I just haven't had the heart to tell him that I wouldn't want to be "fixed" even if he could fix me.

Casey is a unique case. Many of the energy workers I have encountered who have actually recognized my unique spiritual state are not nearly so benign in their attempts to "fix" me. I had one fanatical healer at a New Age convention practically try and throw me onto her massotherapy couch in order to heal what she considered a life-threatening defect. When I quietly explained to her that I was both aware of the defect and did not consider it a problem, she grew patronizing. She told me that I only believed such nonsense because I had grown accustomed to the problem and, having been abnormal for so long, had come to mistake my state for spiritual normalcy. My belief that the condition helped me in any way was only a delusional compensation for the spiritual deficiency I suffered from.

Later in the convention, I found her following me around, trying to heal me from afar. She went so far as to "accidentally" brush up against me in a crowd, trying to sneak in a quick laying-on of hands in the process. Needless to say, she gave me the creeps. It was like knowing that someone, somewhere, is sticking pins in a voodoo doll they've made for you or that little old ladies are crouching over their rosary beads in a church somewhere, praying for the salvation of your soul.

Yet it is almost impossible to escape such judgment. Mainstream culture does not believe in us at all, and the magickal workers who know otherwise only want to fix us or wipe us out entirely. Vampirism, because it is so distrusted and misunderstood carries with it a stigma as heavy as homosexuality. It is our secret, and our greatest burden. As a writer, I am always aware that my secret cannot get out. If my more mainstream publishers were to learn what I believed myself to be, I fully expect that they would drop me from their companies. Vampirism is a stain in their eyes. It is either indicative of a severe mental disorder or it is patently evil. Admitting to being a vampire invalidates all the other good qualities you have. Everything becomes tainted by association. No matter what your other qualities as a person, no matter how valuable the work you do might be, the stigma of vampirism would overshadow everything. Just consider poor Oscar Wilde.

Oscar Wilde was a poet and revered playwright from the late nineteenth century. During his lifetime, Wilde's homosexuality became public knowledge through a lawsuit levied against him by the father of one of his lovers. Wilde was not only incarcerated for this. His wife and children left the country and assumed a different name so as not to be associated with his stigma. His sons were never told much about their father, and it was many, many years before they learned the dark secret that landed their father in the labor camp that wrecked his health and led to his death. His plays, consistent hits on the London stage, were dropped when news of his orientation spread. His writings were condemned, and even the mention of his name in anything but a negative light was enough to bring the speaker under suspicion of homosexuality himself. Oscar spent his last days as a virtual vagabond in Europe, a ragged pauper broken in body and spirit. He never wrote again. What use was it to write? He knew that his talent was of no value to the public eye -- not when viewed in contrast with his hideous sexual orientation.

I am painfully aware of Wilde's position. It is the position I find myself in, especially now that I have released *The Psychic Vampire Codex* to the general market. In outing my vampirism, I am inviting the scorn and condemnation of hundreds of readers. The Pagans and the Religious Right may be diametrically opposed to one another in all other things, but they share common ground in their condemnation of vampires. And yet I have faith that what I have chosen to do with my life and my talent is something very necessary. Just as gays began making inroads into modern culture by telling their stories, fighting for acceptance in a world that held them guilty simply for existing, someone has to make the first case for the vampire. Who else is going to get the information about us out there so everyone can find it? How else can we dispel all the negative myths and rumors except to publish our truths?

Why Vampires?

Many of my articles have been written exclusively for publication on the Internet. This is such a one, and it has been reprinted on several sites, including the widely read ***Sanguinarius.org****, a non-partisan site that has provided sane and reliable information for real vampires since the 1990s. It was most recently reprinted in the September 2005 edition of Shadowlore's newsletter,* ***The Shadow Tymes.***

I've done more interviews than I can count in the past few years, and in almost every case, the first question I'm asked is, "So why do you call yourself a *vampire*?"

The fact of the matter is, it comes down to life. Throughout the folklore, the qualities attributed to vampires vary widely. In Romanian myth alone, as cited by folklorist Harry Senn in *The Were-Wolf and Vampire in Romania*, there are living vampires in addition to the more traditional undead variety. Some can walk abroad during the day. Some feed directly from victims, while others can suck blood from many miles away. Still other folkloric vampires drain the milk from herds of cows or drain the very life from a field of grain.

The one consistent quality of the vampire is its need for life, for the vital force. Throughout my life, I have evidenced a need to regularly and actively take vital energy from those around me in order to maintain my physical, mental, and spiritual well-being. We have no better word in the English language for this taking than vampirism, and this makes me, by default, a vampire -- whether I like the word or not.

The vampire, as it has developed in the modern imagination, is a being who is immortal, fears the sun, has rejected or is rejected by all things hallowed and holy, and who drinks blood. Garlic and cloaks, fangs and pale skin are usually mixed up in there as well, as is the propensity to sleep in a coffin, fly, shapeshift, and be destroyed by a stake through the heart.

A real vampire, like myself, has a need for life energy - though this is not necessarily expressed through the drinking of blood. I don't sleep in a coffin or transform into a bat. I haven't tried the stake through the heart thing, though I'm willing to bet it would hurt, and kill me just as dead as the next person.

I do tend to be nocturnal, and I am sensitive to the sun and bright light - but I'm exceptionally sensitive to all forms of energy. Some, like UV radiation, make me sick - tired, lethargic, nauseated, if I'm over-exposed. Others, I just interfere with - the last documentary team that worked with me was a little surprised when they couldn't keep batteries charged around me, and when I toured last fall with my band, we learned I couldn't get my hand near a microphone without getting some nasty feedback. Radio and television reception, touch lighting, and DSL connections all behave strangely around me. Friends, family, co-workers -- anyone who spends any amount of time around me comes to accept such phenomena as fact simply because instances occur so often as to be commonplace.

As for the powers of the vampire - the immortality - my mom can attest that I've remembered my past lives since I was a kid. This isn't in the strictest sense immortality, but it definitely gives me an ageless perspective, and I do feel it's connected with my vampirism (this "serial immortality" is common among members of the vampire community).

I'm an empath with some degree of telepathy, and there is an aura about me, an allure that can be equated with the mesmerism of the vampire. In general, people react one of two ways to this aura of mine: they're either fascinated or they're frightened. Psychics and other sensitives pick up on it quickly and in a very conscious way. However, even people who would swear that they don't have a psychic bone in their body will respond to this energy I have, though they don't seem to think too hard about where their impressions are coming from.

Of course, just to feed even more into the archetype, especially as it's been established in television and film today, I'm tall, thin, pale, and attractive - though this is easily attributable to good genes than to vampirism, as two of my aunts were rather successful fashion models back in the seventies.

Now personally, I hate the word "vampire" and would like nothing more than to divorce myself from it completely. It has caused innumerable problems in my public and my private life, and whenever it comes up as the first thing someone knows about me, I know I'm going to have an uphill battle in getting them to accept me for me.

So why do I even cater to such an ill-fitting word if it's generated so much grief? Well, for a while I fought against it and all the trappings that came with it, but there was this incident at the mall. I was dressed as normally as anyone else there, t-shirt, blue jeans, some turquoise jewelry. There was not a stitch of black clothing on me -- if anything, I could have posed for the cover of some New Age magazine. But as I walked through the food court, this little girl's head turns and with wide, amazed eyes, she follows me. Pointing now, she tugs on her mother's clothes and utters, clear as day, "Mommy! Look at the vampire!"

Had this been an isolated incident, I'd just brush it off as a weird coincidence. But it happened more than once – at the museum, at the park, at the mall -- so often, in fact, that there was simply no denying it. Something about what that word means to people fits me. Even when they have no clues as to what they're looking at and no good reason to connect that word with me, it still surfaces. When an archetype is so thoroughly ingrained in the collective unconscious and so obviously connected in some way to me, there's no sense in fighting it.

Or, as one friend long ago quipped, *"If the cape fits, wear it."*

THE MODERN VAMPIRE COMMUNITY

When noted Wiccan author Kerr Cuhulain contacted me for help on the vampire chapter in his law-enforcement guide to the occult community, I was very enthusiastic. In addition to placing my private collection of vampire texts at his disposal, I wrote extensive notes on the history and development of the vampire subculture. With a little tweaking, those notes developed into the article you see below on the history and development of the modern community.

The vampire makes his first appearance in Western literature in the poem "Der Vampir" by German author, Heinrich August Ossenfelder, in 1748. The figure of the vampire was then taken up by the Romantic poet Lord Byron in the early 1800s, whose influence upon Polidori's book, *The Vampyre*, firmly established the archetype in the literature of the English-speaking world.

On a less literary note, psychic vampires are first referred to in the Flying Rolls (instructional texts) of the Hermetic Order of the Golden Dawn (1890s). The concept is later elaborated upon by Dion Fortune in *Psychic Self* Defense (1930). Some conjecture persists that certain historical figures, most notably the actor Sir Henry Irving and the poet Lord Byron, exhibited qualities that identify them as psychic vampires. There is evidence that their vampiric qualities were significant enough to inspire people close to them to fictionalize them as vampires. Byron appears as Lord Ruthven in Polidori's *The Vampyre*. Sir Henry Irving in part inspired Bram Stoker's famous Count Dracula. However, insufficient primary evidence exists to prove these conjectures beyond the shadow of a doubt.

What we do know is that as early as the nineteenth century, particularly within the magickal movement, there were individuals who were recognized as vampiric. This was not vampirism in the strict folkloric sense, but its metaphysical cousin, as these living vampires did not feed upon blood but upon the subtle energies of the life force, variously described as "psychic energy," "etheric energy" and a whole host of colorful terms.

The vampirism of these individuals was generally looked upon as an affliction and was thought to be something beyond their conscious control. The idea that an individual could be vampiric and could embrace this quality consciously, even harnessing it to become a significant and empowering

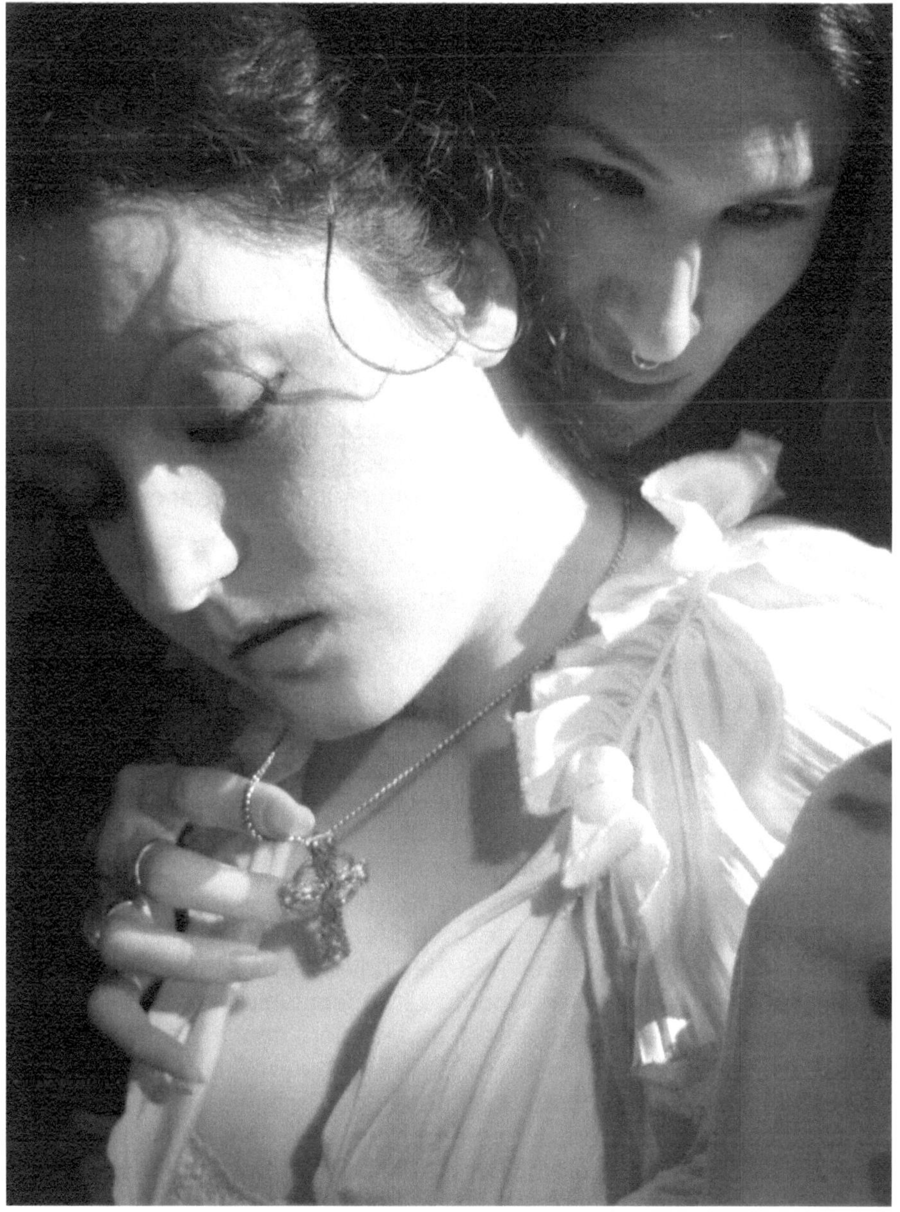

part of their personal identity does not seem to have occurred until the latter half of the twentieth century.

Modern vampires began to embrace and explore their natures as early as the 1960s. A possible influence on the vampire's transformation from an horrific creature of myth to a romantic pop-culture anti-hero was the television series *Dark Shadows*. This ground-breaking Gothic soap opera portrayed a sympathetic vampire in the figure of Barnabas Collins. Sympathetic portrayals of vampires in fiction and film opened the door for individuals to conceptualize the vampire as something other than hated and evil. The novels of Anne Rice furthered the idea of the vampire as a potentially sympathetic being.

At this time, individuals with vampiric qualities began experimenting with what those qualities meant to them personally and spiritually. By 1970, there was no formalized vampire community per se, but there were several movements that allowed for at least a minimal expression of one's vampiric traits. In the underground fetish scene, particularly in New York City, many individuals recognized the energetic exchange between dom and sub. Blood play was also accepted, and so both psychic and sanguine vampires found an outlet for some of their needs here. In the Gothic subculture, the vampire was seen as a romantic figure whose personal magnetism, power, and immortality appealed greatly to men and women alike. Awakening vampires were subsequently drawn to this community because it was acceptable to style yourself after the vampire, and the Gothic movement in turn allowed them to further explore dark aesthetics and philosophies that appealed to them.

Many vampires were also drawn to the Pagan movement. This allowed them to acknowledge the spiritual side of their natures. Pagans and vampires both share beliefs in magick, reincarnation, and the existence of energy. Finally, *Vampire: the Masquerade*, which itself was inspired by the novels of Anne Rice, provided a social venue where vampires could experiment with their identities without fear of ridicule. Although vampires understood the games to be make-believe, they nevertheless attracted individuals with an interest in vampires and the occult, a fact which in turn allowed people with shared interests to connect and explore those common interests outside of the game.

Because the vampire community developed within several different preestablished communities, once it emerged as a full-fledged community unto itself, it remained indelibly stamped with influences from the various groups it was born from. Much of the interaction between vampire and donor holds lingering traces of the dom/sub relationship from BDSM. (This is especially evident in the Elorathian treatment of the Kitra caste where donors are frequently depicted as BDSM slaves.) Vampires borrowed many of their aesthetics from the Gothic movement and this is reflected in the music, art, and fashion one encounters at any vampire community event. Much of the vampire community's fundamental understanding of magick and ritual is derived from modern Paganism, and this is particularly noticeable in the shared paradigm of an eight-holiday Wheel of the Year.

Finally, a great deal of the initial social structure as well as certain terms show the influence of *Vampire: the Masquerade*. *V:tM* developed a live-action version of its table-top game, which was essentially improvisational theater set in the fictional vampires' "World of Darkness." It was through these "Live Action" games that many vampires first began socializing with one another openly. Thus, despite the popularity of the term "house" to describe a group of vampires, one will sometimes still encounter the word "clan" and several terms for various vampiric abilities, such as "presence," hearken back to the language established by the role-playing game.

Despite these many various influences, the vampire subculture has evolved over the years into a viable and unique community that stands as a movement in its own right, with new groups, concepts, and traditions being established every year. On the whole, the development of the vampire community can be approached as a fascinating example of how a vibrant and living tradition can develop in the modern world today.

Vampires on Parade

*Written in early 2004, this was another article published originally to **disinfo.com** in response to the interest generated by SciFi's **Mad, Mad House**. A number of vampire sites have reprinted the article, and a version of it can also be found on **kheperu.org**.*

With the huge fan-base developed by shows like *Buffy* and its sexy spin-off *Angel*, vampires are a hot topic these days. The vampires of fiction and film have long chilled and thrilled us, but now interest has grown in another aspect of this many-faceted archetype: the vampire as a reality.

It sounds like the plot of a new television series, but it's the truth: Lurking just beneath the normal veneer of mainstream society is another, shadowy world. It is the underground world of the real vampire. In North and South America, throughout Europe, Australia and even Japan, a hidden network of clubs, havens, houses, and secret qabals cater to the vampire community. In back rooms and private VIP lounges, real vampires gather, enjoy one another's company, celebrate their culture, and feed.

CSI: Vegas's vampire episode aired in February 2004, and SciFi's reality TV show *Mad, Mad House* have brought the reality of the vampire to living rooms across America. And Americans, enthralled by these dark and sexy people, want to know more.

Vampire History

For years, the real vampire community has existed in the shadows. For many, discretion and secrecy were the keys to survival, and widespread codes of conduct, such as the internationally-known Black Veil, grew up to provide guidelines of behavior for veterans and newcomers alike. Advances in technology like the Internet, an increasingly tolerant (and curious) culture, and increased cooperation among the vampires themselves have all combined in recent years to "out" this fascinating community to the mainstream.

There is a definite Gothic element to the most visible portion of the subculture, but don't let this retro aesthetic fool you. The eighties and nineties saw the vampire subculture make huge strides in becoming a community as independent groups started reaching out and communicating with one another. However, real vampires were alive and well long before that.

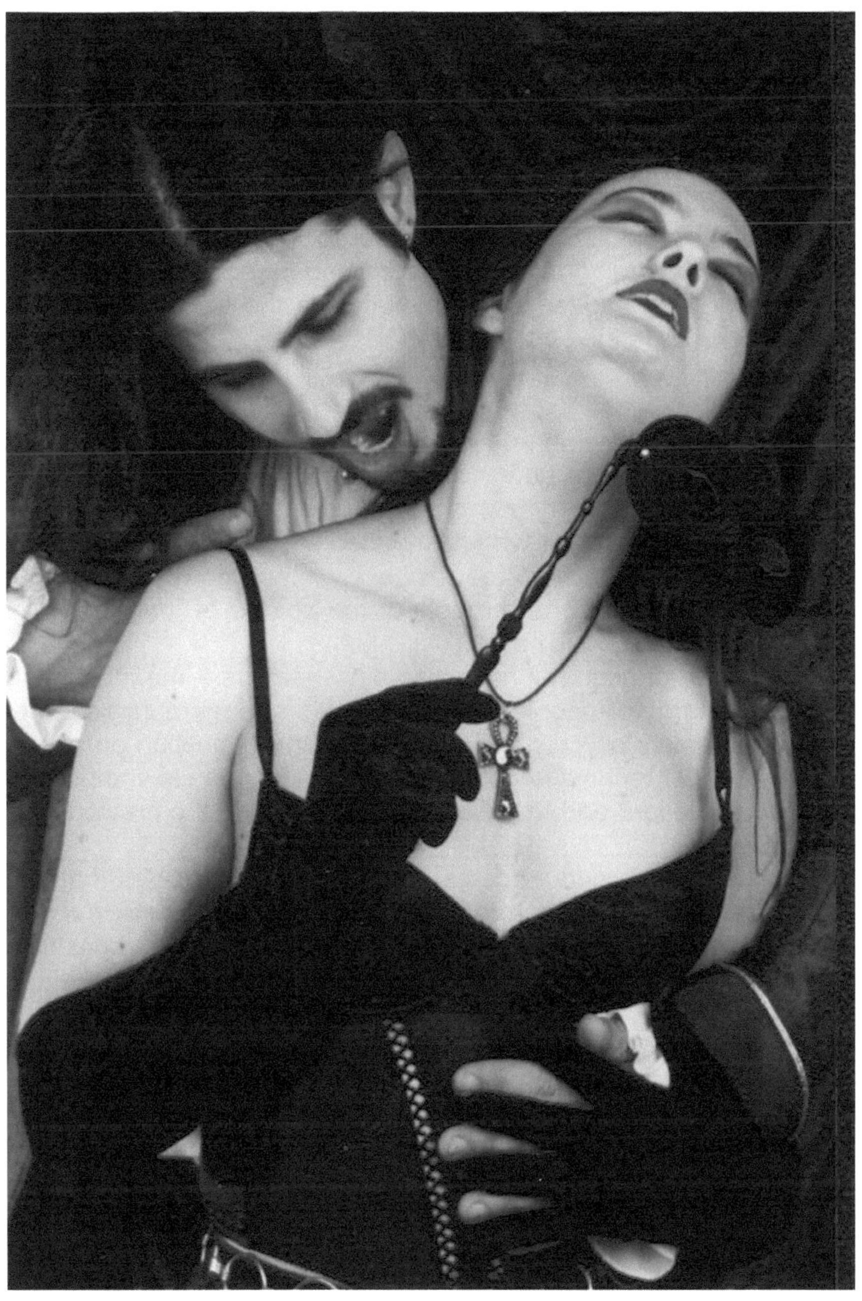

According to the Goddess Rosemary, mentor of the Sanguinarium's Father Sebastian, vampire groups were active in New York City as early as the nineteen sixties, often interwoven throughout that era's thriving fetish underground. Rosemary's code-word for these early vamps is "Azralim," a term later taken up by her student in his book, *V,* and depicted as the true secret underground of vampire society.

Going well beyond New York of the Twentieth Century, occultist Aleister Crowley, who lived from 1875 to 1947, seems to have practiced a form of psi and sang vampirism almost identical to that taught in *The Psychic Vampire Codex*. According to material compiled by occult researcher Francis King, Crowley had added these methods to the tractates of the Ordo Templi Orientis prior to the First World War.

Meet the Vampire

So real, live vampires, in and of themselves, are nothing new. But the fact that many of them are now willing to come forward and explain what they are is a very recent phenomenon.

One vampire in particular who has placed himself in the spotlight is the vampire Don Henrie. Don was the resident vampire on the first season of SciFi's *Mad, Mad House,* and throughout the course of that show, he revealed many truths about his nature.

Don is a blood-drinker, but he is also a psi-vampire -- meaning he feeds upon the vital energy of people through psychic and metaphysical means. Don is also extremely psychic and practices astral projection on an almost nightly basis. Other techniques he uses that draw upon his vampire nature such as "augmentation" and "manifesting" are taught in the previously mentioned *Codex*.

Don acknowledges and respects codes like the Black Veil that caution discretion in revealing one's nature. Yet Don is not one to hide in the shadows, and he would like to see a day where other vampires like himself could feel comfortable letting the world know they exist and are not likely to go away.

Lost in the Shadows

Many traditionalists within the vampire community are resistant to such a policy of openness. Some fear for their personal privacy, as many have jobs, friendships, or family connections that might suffer if their nature were to be revealed. Others are afraid that there could be much deeper and far-reaching repercussions if the community went public.

They have some valid concerns. People have lost jobs, had their children taken away, and even been brutally attacked just because of their vampirism. When so little information is widely available on the reality of vampires, it is easy for people outside of the community to pass judgment and lash out toward that which they do not understand.

And yet Don Henrie, and others like him, have a salient point to make. The fear and hatred experienced by mainstream society toward real vampires typically arise from ignorance of what vampires really are. And by lurking in the shadows, real vampires are not likely to help make such ignorance disappear. It is only by making the public aware of the vampire community that any manner of constructive dialogue can begin.

By appearing on *Mad, Mad House,* Don Henrie took the initiative to start that dialogue. For good or for ill, thanks to him, a spotlight now shines on the real vampire community. That spotlight makes it almost impossible to slip back into the shadows again. Even for those who will stubbornly remain in the underground, the public is now aware that such an underground exists. Joe Average might not understand vampires completely, but he will be looking over his shoulder the next time he's at a club or local bar wondering, “Is he one of them? Is she?” Eventually, there will be no hiding anymore.

Out of the Coffin

The vampire community is vast and extensively diverse. Don Henrie, by his own admission, represents just one portion of that community, and when it comes down to it, he can really only share his own perceptions on what being a vampire really means. But for other voices and points of view to be heard, others within the vampire subculture have to step forward.

There was a time when you couldn't be gay and be open about. There was a time when you couldn't be a witch and be open about. Maybe the time has come that you can be a vampire and be open about it. Don Henrie seems to think that time is now. And only time will tell if others share enough conviction to add their voices to his own.

In Defense of Psi-Vamps

Over the years, I have written a great deal of what amounts to vampire apologetics. This particular article, published to my site ***kheperu.org*** *in 2002, was penned in response to a letter received from a psivamp who had stirred up trouble for himself by outing his nature to his Wiccan High Priestess. Although written primarily from a psi-vamp's point of view, I have had the satisfaction of seeing this article referenced on several Wiccan forums and websites.*

It is a common belief among Pagans -- and Wiccans in particular -- that psychic vampirism is an aberration or an outright crime. It is understood to be something done willfully by the psi-vamp, and it is seen as something typically done for power, self-indulgence, or maliciousness. While there are certainly individuals who engage in learned vampirism for pleasure or sport, the existence of such persons in no ways invalidates the reality of those who have an actual and legitimate energetic need.

Those Pagans and/or Wiccans who are willing to accept the notion that some people may naturally require the taking of energy will typically draw the line at human vital energy (widely known as *chi*) with the reasoning that there are all kinds of energy people can tap into, so a psi-vamp should be able to go out and basically eat a tree.

So what is a psychic vampire if not someone who is addicted to the taking of energy or who takes it simply because they can?

Some people do not naturally produce enough vital energy to sustain optimal physical, spiritual, and mental well-being. Such individuals must actively take energy from the environment around them to supplement their personal vital energy.

If such a person is able to consistently draw upon the energy of nature, the earth, celestial energy, elemental energy or some other outside source that *does not include* other people, then he or she is what I'd label a partial psi-vamp. Such a person can sustain their physical, mental, and spiritual well-being without taking the vital life force from other people, but he or she still has a distinct energetic need.

Now, a full-blown psi-vamp is an individual who has this energetic need but is additionally *limited* almost exclusively to sustaining themselves through the vital energy of other people, This can be taken through sexual interactions, it can be taken ambiently from crowds, it can be taken in the form of emotional energy, and some will take it through the medium of blood.

The defining factor of a full-blown psi-vamp is that the vampire cannot adequately sustain his or her basic physical, mental, and spiritual well-being by taking any outside energy *except for* human vital energy. This person will need to actively take such energy on a semi-regular basis (once a week to once a month on average, depending on activity, metabolism, severity of need, etc.,) or else suffer a loss of overall health as a result.

To be cut off from such energy will cause general lethargy, depression of the immune system, and a host of other ills.

Now, in defense of the Pagans who have formulated such a negative opinion of us, it is certainly true that unconscious psychic vampires who have no idea what they are doing can be exceptionally destructive to those around them. Typically, a lot of unawakened psi-vamps will unconsciously create emotionally charged and melodramatic situations expressly to feed off of the energy which results. They are attention-getters, drama queens and oh poor me's.

The untrained and unawakened tend to be in the vast majority, so it's from experiences with these that most metaphysicians have formulated their opinions of psychic vampires as a whole. And having had to deal with some stubbornly unawakened psi-vamps, I can understand to a point where they're coming from. Such people are indeed a royal pain in the butt.

However, the fact that such poor souls exist is no good reason to reject the entire community as a whole, nor is it reason to judge all of us by someone's bad behavior. Psi-vampirism is a very real phenomenon, and it is often as difficult for the awakening psi-vamp to realize that he or she has an actual and legitimate need for human energy which is tied in directly to his or her health as it is for a Pagan, Wiccan, or New Ager to accept that for some people, only a very limited spectrum of energy can sustain them at all.

Those who object to the very existence of psychic vampires should not attempt to obscure the subject or suppress what little information is available to those awakening to what they are. Instruction and awareness are the two best tools to combat those pesky psi-vamps that run around creating headaches for everyone.

Taking energy from an unwilling target is indeed unethical. But someone who is unaware of what they are doing and how to control it cannot adequately make an ethical decision about how and when they feed. Learning to consciously take energy is the only thing that will enable a true psi-vamp to make ethical decisions about their feeding habits. Once they have achieved awareness and self-control, then they can harness what they are more positively, seeking out willing and able donors instead of randomly taking energy from anyone who crosses into their space.

Far too often well-meaning friends and mentors tell a psychic vampire that their need is not real, that it's all in their heads, or that it's some manner of learned addiction. However, this advice, no matter how well-intentioned, only prevents them from achieving the understanding that they need to develop a healthy approach to who and what they are. Rather than judging or discounting someone's vampirism, the best course of action is to be supportive in helping them understand their nature so they can choose an ethical way of meeting their needs.

Vampirism as Identity

A number of my articles have been inspired either by letters written directly to me or, more often, by questions raised on the vampire-related e-lists and forums that I run. The following article was written in 2001, and it developed out of a discussion on why so many modern vampires are driven to adopt the characteristics of their undead folkloric and literary counterparts.

Vampirism as defined in the modern community it is really just a condition of the soul or energy body typified by a heightened need for energy. It's not really an identity so much as it is a characteristic some people happen to share. In many respects, it may be less misleading to say that someone is *vampiric* rather than simply calling them a vampire. Someone who is vampiric merely shares some qualities with vampires as we understand them. And yet what about those people who proudly proclaim themselves to be *vampires*? Why do they feel the need to integrate some of the more mythic qualities of the vampire into their daily lives?

Even though modern vampirism is technically nothing more than a need for vital energy, people often choose to define themselves as vampires in much the same way that people choose to define themselves as left-handed. Being left-handed is just one characteristic a person may have. They could be male or female, black or white, but for whatever reason, they choose the label "Southpaw" when defining themselves. They think of themselves as "lefties". They buy little books like *The Left-Hander's Guide to Everything.* They wear T-shirts that proclaim them to be left-handed. They use special pencils or other tools that cater to their inherent left-handedness.

Some people take it a bit far. When your entire house is redone with left-handedness in mind, it's probably gone *way* too far. But people do just the same thing with vampirism. Sometimes it's a matter of accepting it in themselves -- I've met some left-handed people who are pretty bitter that they live in a right-handed world. So they make it a point of pride and rebellion to proudly proclaim themselves "lefties." I've met vampires like that. They've really got something to prove, maybe to themselves, maybe to others, so their vampirism affects the way they dress, the jewelry they wear, and virtually every other aspect of their life to a degree that can, at times, seem obsessive.

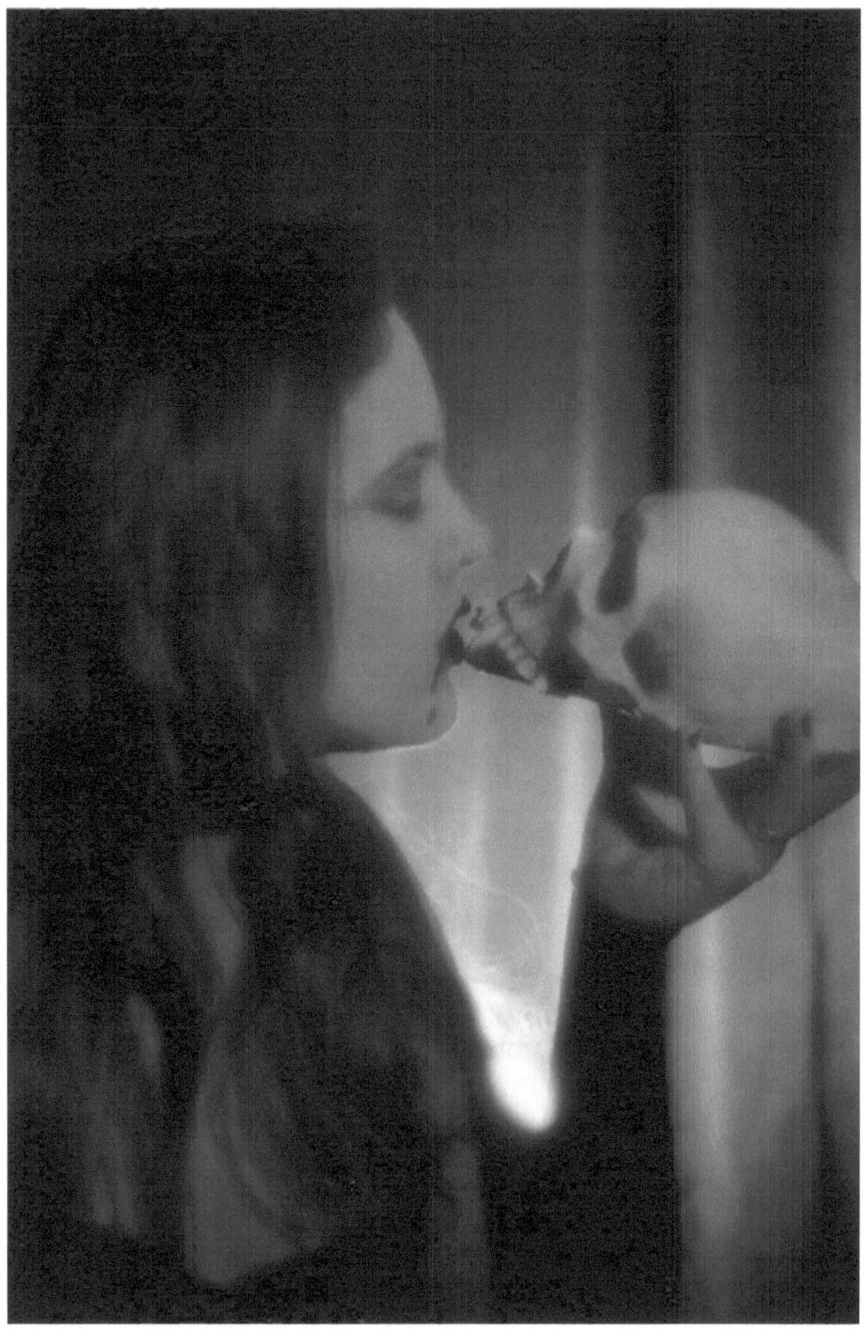

Then there are people who just happen to write with their left hands -- they don't make a big fuss over it, they don't proclaim it to the world, but they'll admit that they're left-handed if you ask. And I've met plenty of vampires like that as well. For them, it's just another aspect of who they are -- nothing to be proud or ashamed about, just a fact of life.

Is either approach good or bad? I think it's a matter of personal choice. People are people, whether they're Southpaws or vampires, and everyone has to find their identity on their own.

At one time, being left-handed was seen as something evil. The French word for left is *sinistre,* and it shares the same Latin root as our English word "sinister." It's funny how myth and legend can make something very simple into something strange and frightening. It was only relatively recently that people became more enlightened about Southpaws and began to understand that left-handed people were not the minions of Satan.

Modern vampires are like the Lefties of ages past. Very little is understood of vampirism, and that lack of understanding makes vampirism seem evil and subversive. Yet every day our culture understands the interaction between energy and vitality more and more. At some point in the future, vampirism may become just as unremarkable as left-handedness -- not a trait everyone shares, but certainly nothing to go waving garlic at.

What's in a Word?

The hot and cold romance that the modern community has had with the word "vampire" might make most people wonder why we haven't come up with a better descriptor for ourselves. I've spilled a great deal of ink over the issue of the v-word, and the following article first appeared on the revised version of my site, ***kheperu.org****, in 2003.*

Although I have appeared on international television and proclaimed myself a vampire, I remain ambivalent toward the v-word. Even after writing the definitive book on modern vampires, *The Psychic Vampire Codex,* I just can't bring myself to feel completely comfortable with that word: *vampire*.

I'll acknowledge that it's the best and most widely understood word for I am, but at the same time, saying the word out loud in connection with myself sometimes just makes me cringe. Or want to laugh. Or just roll my eyes at how pretentious some people make that word seem to outsiders.

Now, there was a time when I embraced the v-word proudly, but that was in that identity-seeking late-teen period when proclaiming myself to be a vampire was almost a dare to myself to believe it. I've come to believe that that's a natural stage people go through in learning to accept something difficult about themselves. I've watched a lot of people go through those stages, and from vampires to Wiccans to gays, I've seen this early period, right after the guilty denial and the tentative acceptance, where the person just throws themselves headlong into that different identity. It's almost like they are trying to convince themselves that this is what they are -- and in order to convince themselves, they go to all manner of extremes with it.

For example, many of my gay friends who are in this stage of self-acceptance tend to put rainbows and p-flags all over their homes. P-flags adorn their clothes, the office cubicles, their cars. They make a point of being out in every aspect of their lives, sometimes to the point of bad taste. Wiccans and Pagans in this stage decorate their homes in neo-Pagan chic. They put pentacles on their cars, pentacles on their cats' collars, they have pentacles dangling from their ears and every other available bit of body-jewelry.

And of course vampires, like every other fringe community, go through

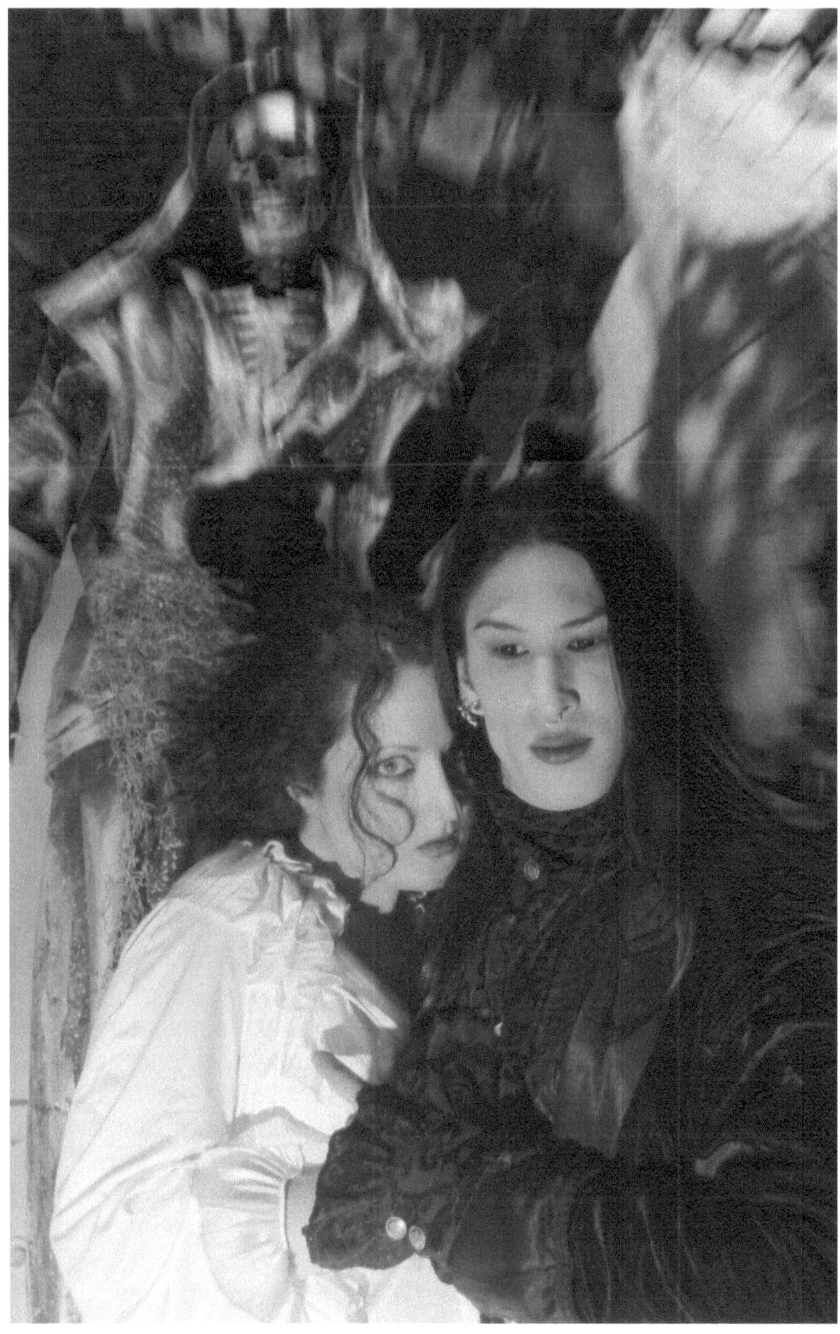

this stage as well. They pale their faces and wear their sunglasses constantly. They hang ankhs around their necks, ankhs from their ears, they get ankh tattoos, bumper stickers, and so on. Some of them go so far as wearing capes and tooth-caps like they were casual wear, not just limiting such attire to clubs, but stomping out to Denny's at eleven o'clock at night in full regalia in spite of and perhaps because of the stares from the local rednecks.

Like a gay couple kissing in the middle of a Southern Baptist Church, this of course is over-kill. And on the surface it looks like it's meant for everyone around that person -- but in reality, that stage is really for *them*. By inundating themselves so thoroughly in that identity, that lifestyle, they are trying to accept it as a reality for themselves. So I think I proudly proclaimed myself a vampire when I was going through that rather awkward stage of only half believing it about myself anyway.

These days, I prefer to see the v-word as a communication tool. It's not the best word for what I and others like me are, but it's the closest word we have in the English language. I know it was the v-word that I was finally drawn to when I first started understanding and coming to terms with my nature. It follows that many others who are just trying to understand themselves will also be drawn to that word. If I'm going to fulfill my mission of reaching out to others like myself and educating them so they can control their vampirism and choose to feed consciously from aware and willing donors, then I have to speak in the language that the majority of people will understand. That includes using words like vampire, psychic vampire, and psi-vamp.

Of course, using the word "vampire" only helps me communicate with people who already understand that it doesn't mean blood-sucking Undead. With all the folkloric and cinematic trappings the image of the vampire has obtained over the years, there's a lot of connotations that come along with the word "vampire" in the popular imagination. It's pretty hard explaining to people outside of the community that we're not laying claim to all of these silly trappings when we define ourselves as vampires. It's kind of like the difficulty the Wiccans had for a long while of convincing the general populace that they didn't ride on broomsticks or wear black, pointy hats.

In more diverse communities, I try to use words that are still descriptive yet lack some of the shock-value that comes with the term "vampire." "Feeder" and "taker" are two terms I've used with some success in describing what we are to New Age and other open-minded spiritual audiences. I do lectures and workshops locally and sometimes at conventions, so I end up dealing with audiences that span the Pagan, Wiccan, New Age, Gothic, and Vampire crowds. Eventually, I hope to be able to get all of these groups communicating in a language they all can understand, so even the most timid white-lighters of the New Age community can understand that vampires are out there, they're not evil, undead, beings, and that the process of taking energy is as natural to some people as giving it is to others.

LOVING THE DEAD: THE ALLURE OF THE MODERN VAMPIRE

This is perhaps my favorite article from the series written for ***disinfo.com*** *in response to the airing of SciFi's* ***Mad, Mad House*** *in the spring of 2004. Although written from the perspective of pop culture, the article allowed me to delve fairly deeply into the psychology of the vampire. As you read this and the other works collected in this book, you will see that it is the psychology of the vampire more than anything else that has allowed it to continue to romance us as an imaginative archetype.*

Angel. Spike. Lestat. Count Dracula. Even when we know they're the bad guys, we love them still. In the past few decades, the vampire has emerged as a pop cultural icon, a being whose image is synonymous with seduction and dark allure. It is exactly this allure that the SciFi network is banking on to sell their living vampire, Don Henrie. And yet the vampire started its life as a creature of horror -- a folkloric boogeyman that terrorized villages and stank of the grave. How has such a monster -- damned and undead -- transformed through the ages into a being of romance and sexual fantasy?

The vampire as it exists in the modern imagination is just one facet of an enduring archetype: the eternal outsider. As an archetypal figure, the vampire exists outside the bounds of normative reality. Superficially, he is a part of the human race, but he is always apart from it. While his nature makes him an outcast, both the vampire's power and his allure arise from this outcast state. The Romantic ideal of Lucifer as the rebellious angel taps into this archetype as well. It is the Byronic dark hero, the quintessential "bad boy" who thrills and seduces us because he breaks the rules. Consider the wild popularity of Anne Rice's vampire Lestat. People find such a liminal being sexy, mysterious, and darkly compelling.

The evolution of the vampire from a corpse-like bloodsucker to a seductive bad boy occurred long before Lestat or any of the others came on the scene. The romantic ideal of the vampire goes back to the poet Lord Byron (1788-1824). A passionate and complicated man, Byron was the living embodiment of the eternal outsider, and he knew it. Throughout his career, he identified himself with other mythic outcasts: the fallen angel

Shemyaza; Lucifer; the Biblical Cain. When he ran across the notion of the vampire, it was a natural fit for someone who never quite felt a part of humanity.

Byron first encountered the idea of the vampire during his coming-of-age travels in Greece. At that time, the vampire was a very real thing to the Greek peasantry. Fascinated by all things occult and macabre, Byron learned all he could about these nightly predators, thrilled by them as much as he was thrilled by tales of ghosts and demons. But what connected him psychologically to the vampire of folklore was again its outsider status: it was widely believed that one became a vampire through some fall from grace or other misdeed. Byron felt he himself had been foredoomed to wickedness through some vague but terrible past deed, and so the vampire was added to his repertoire of damned beings.

Had the vampire merely remained a private obsession of Byron's, the creature may never had grown into the pop cultural icon it is today. However, Byron's personal physician, a young Italian by the name of John William Polidori, fell in love with Byron and grew to hate him for that illicit love. As an expression of his hatred, Polidori wrote a novella, *The Vampyre*, which featured Lord Byron under the guise of Lord Ruthven, the evil, immortal title character.

Polidori tried very hard to make Ruthven seem like a heartless monster, but his own mixed feelings toward Byron imbued the character with a peculiar commingling of sadism and humanity. Ruthven, like Byron, was a tortured being, monstrous yet vulnerable, fiercely arrogant and tenderly loving by turns. And thus our modern image of the vampire emerged - not the revenant of folklore who is little more than a ravening ghoul, but the vampire as a charismatic and cultured gentleman, whose seductive allure is the ruin of everyone around him.

Stoker, Rice and all the rest merely picked up where Polidori left off, shaping their beautiful monsters on the bones of Lord Ruthven. Rice's frequent allusions to Byron throughout her works are a conscious acknowledgement of the role the poet played in birthing the archetype that gave rise to Lestat.

The archetype of the vampire is a potent one. The self-same fire that burns at the heart of Rice's "brat prince" also enflames the allure of individuals who consciously adopt the archetype in their personal lives.

It is the heady mixture of sex and danger, mystery and revelation that gives individuals like the vampire Don Henrie such a fascinating appeal -- even to those who don't believe in the objective reality of their vampirism. Even before SciFi's *Mad, Mad House* aired, Don Henrie fan sites were popping up all over the 'net. When Don Henrie appeared in a chat on SciFi.

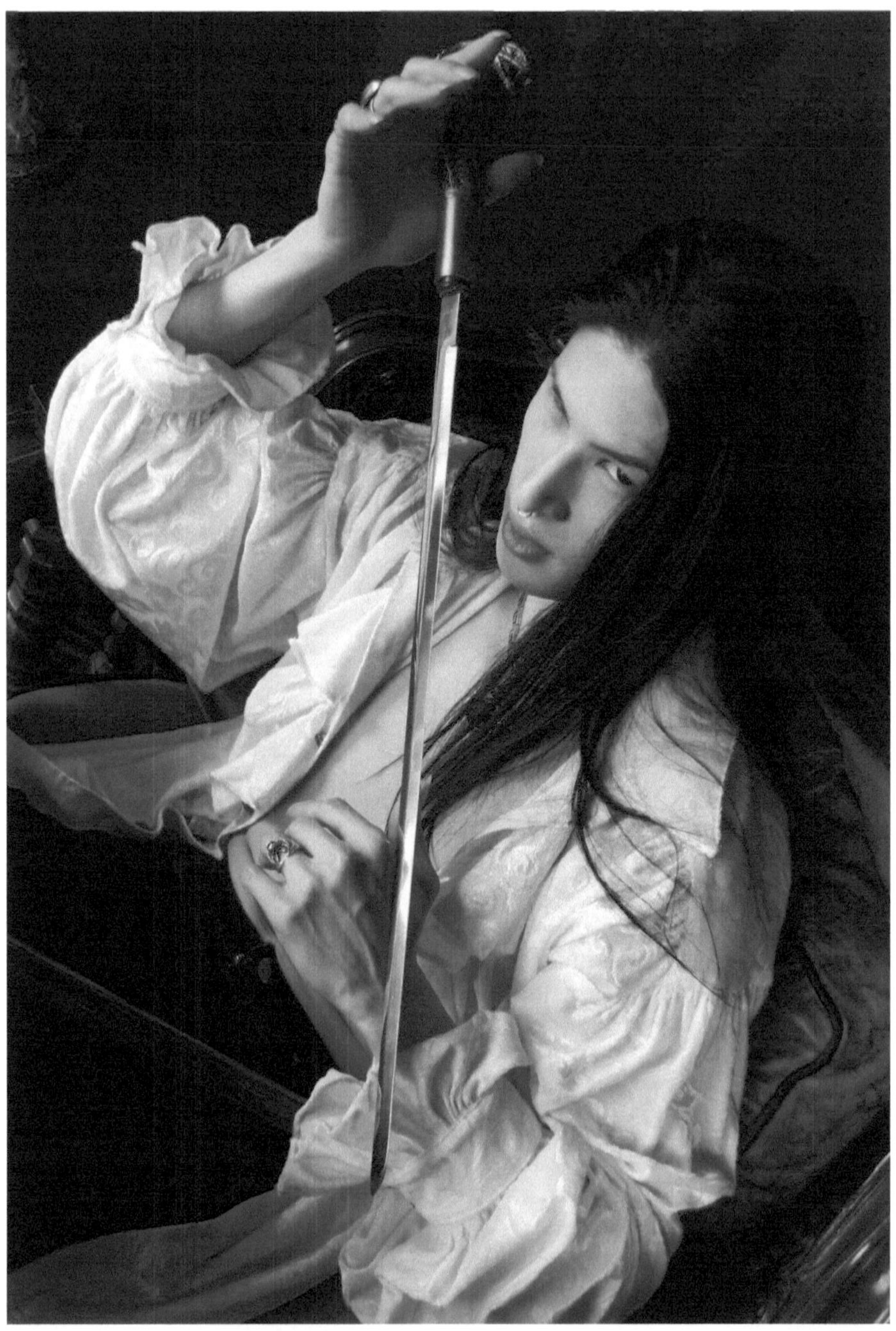

com to promote the show, starry-eyed fans -- boys and girls alike -- gathered for a chance to hear the vampire speak. Once the regulated portion of the chat was over, many fans lingered in the room, dreamily discussing what it would be like to be romanced by a real vampire.

It is hardly surprising, then, that despite debates on the legitimacy of his alternative lifestyle (especially when compared to recognized religions such as Wicca or Voodoo), Don Henrie was one of the most-watched "alts" on the SciFi reality TV show. Regardless of whether or not fans believe him to be an actual living vampire, Don Henrie still taps into that potently alluring archetype. In his manners and in his dress, he is a modern inheritor of the legacy of Byron. Like Byron -- and all the vampires the poet inspired -- Don romances us by daring to break the rules of dayside society and revel in the dark pleasures that everyone else fears to embrace.

The Lord of Vampires

Reading through the previous articles, it's fairly obvious that I am fascinated by the life of the Romantic poet, Lord Byron. I have long suspected that Byron was a psychic vampire, and that the poet himself was at least partially aware of this. In article after article, I danced around this supposition, until finally, in January 2005, I published an article in ***Fate Magazine*** *that directly addressed the issue. That article is reprinted here, with kind permission.*

There is a vampire figure that predates the appearance of *Dracula* by nearly eighty years. The vampire Lord Ruthven is a cold and heartless member of the undead based largely on the living poet Lord Byron. Featured in *The Vampyre* by John William Polidori, Lord Ruthven highlights all of the conflicted and diabolical qualities that made Byron infamous in English society during his lifetime.

Polidori had been Byron's personal physician in the early 1800s, and the relationship between the two men was stormy at best. When Polidori left Byron's service, it was not on good terms, and the strain between the two men was made even worse when Polidori published *The Vampyre* in 1819. In part, this was because *The Vampyre* was originally published under Byron's name, presumably to capitalize on his notoriety. However, the striking similarities between the living Byron and the fictional Ruthven suggest that Polidori had revenge in mind when penning the tale. It was not long after the publication of *The Vampyre* that vampirism was added to the list of unholy crimes supposedly committed by the rakish young lord who had been born George Noel Gordon on January 22, 1788.

Yet Lord Byron had been connected with vampires and vampirism even before Polidori published his famous book. Terribly fascinated with Oriental legends and folklore, Byron himself had first encountered vampire beliefs during his youthful tour of Greece -- a country then riddled with vampire superstitions. The folklore of Greece infected his imagination, giving rise to such memorable lines as these from his poem, "The Giaour:"

But first, on earth as vampire sent,
Thy corpse shall from its tomb be rent
And ghastly haunt thy native place
And suck the blood of all thy race.

Speaking from a literary point of view, Byron is the father of the modern vampire. Polidori shamelessly patterned his vampire Lord Ruthven after Byron, and it was the poet's unique and conflicted spirit that made *The Vampyre's* title character the kind of being that transcends the limits of Polidori's often melodramatic little book. Yet how much of Polidori's character Ruthven grew out of fiction and how much was based on fact? Few students of nineteenth century literature would dare to take the leap necessary to suggest that Byron himself was in some sense vampiric. Yet there are compelling details in Lord Byron's life that suggest the vampire of fiction had some basis in fact.

It is well known that Byron was superstitious, and his involvement in the occult was infamous in his day. He was reported to hold Black Masses at his residence at Newstead Abbey, and among his collected poems there remains a verse he had inscribed upon a chalice fashioned from a human skull. He was also known to keep a collection of skulls in a coffin deep in the bowels of the old abbey. Yet Byron was a flamboyant man who often indulged in macabre and melodramatic acts purely to shock those around him. There were countless rumors about the poet's wild exploits, and he himself enlarged upon many of these.

Because Byron could be such a trickster where his own beliefs were concerned, it is very difficult to know how much of his occult dabblings he actually took seriously. At various times in his poetry, prose, and letters, he identified himself with a wide range of outcast, diabolical figures, including the fallen angel Shemyaza, the Biblical murderer Cain, and the Prince of Darkness himself, Lucifer. But again, it is unclear how much he did this to shock, and how much he himself saw these archetypal figures as descriptive of his nature in some important way.

A close look into Byron's personal life indicates that the poet certainly had some kind of secret -- and this secret was possibly occult in nature. After Byron died, his close friend John Hobhouse burned his memoirs because he felt these revealed too many controversial things about the poet's life. Most scholars presume that the memoirs were committed to the flames in order to cover up records of Byron's sexual indiscretions. And yet all of England was aware of Byron's pursuits in the bedroom, including the incest committed with his half-sister, Augusta. Byron himself had made no secret of his early loss of innocence (at the tender age of seven), and it was widely understood that his appetites drew him to men as well as women (a homosexual liaison gone sour has been given for the real reason behind Polidori's bitter break with his patient).

Since Byron's bedroom habits were practically tabloid affairs, it's hard to see how his memoirs could have shocked English society any further.

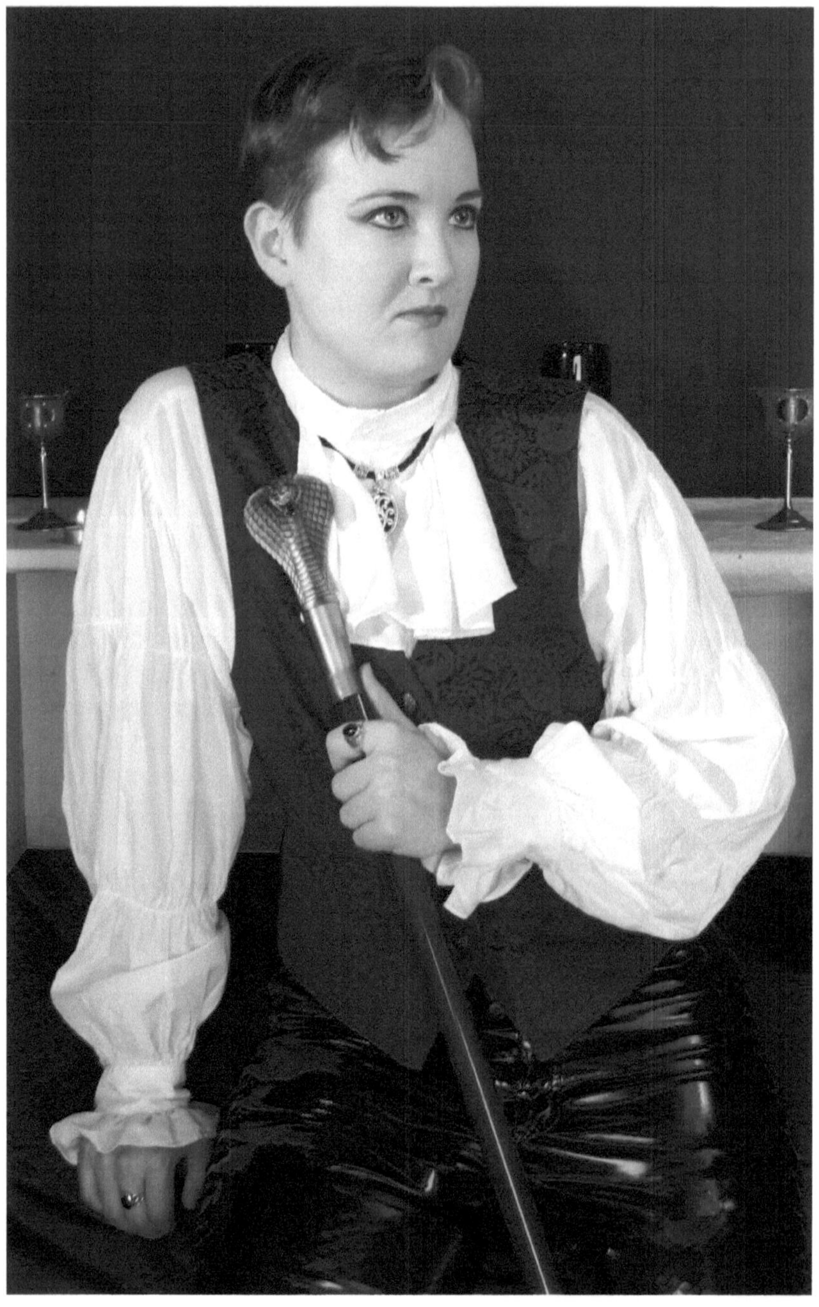

One possible alternative is that Byron's memoirs contained revelatory material concerning Byron's beliefs and practices in the occult. Since he had never publicly owned up to these in his lifetime, Hobhouse may have thought it better that such things went with Byron to the grave. Considering Byron's own words regarding the memoirs, an occult – if not outright vampiric – interpretation seems unavoidable. According to Byron, he withheld a few key details in the memoirs out of deference "to the living, to the dead, and *for those that must be both.*"

One of the periods in his life undoubtedly enlarged upon in the now-lost memoirs was that of the so-called "Haunted Summer" spent in the Swiss Alps at the Villa Diodati in 1816. Byron had fled England in the midst of scandal, leaving behind his wife and infant daughter, Ada Augusta. He stayed at the villa with Polidori, and later they were joined by the poet Percy Bysshe Shelley and his paramour, the future Mary Shelley. Tagging along with this Bohemian pair was Mary's half-sister, Claire Clairmont who – unbeknownst to everyone – was pregnant with Byron's child from an earlier encounter.

A great deal of speculation has been made as to the precise content of the many conversations Byron had with his guests during their stay at the Swiss villa. Various writers and historians have suggested that evenings at Byron's residence included anything from opium-inspired orgies to bloody Satanic rites. Certainly Byron and his guests passed their time flirting with the occult. A now famous contest for creating the most frightening ghost story gave birth to early versions of both Polidori's *The Vampyre* and Mary Shelley's *Frankenstein.* These clearly show that, if nothing else, matters of life, death, and immortality, were staples of the nightly conversations held at the villa. Yet there may have been more than simple dinner conversation going on that rainy summer: at one point during their stay, something scared Percy Shelley so badly that he fled the house in the midst of a dangerous lightning storm. By some accounts, he was stark naked.

Another intriguing detail that strongly argues in favor of a factual tie between Byron and vampirism is the fact that the poet went out of his way to acquire John William Polidori as his personal physician. That Byron needed a personal physician is not in doubt; he had been born with a clubbed foot, and despite numerous and rather agonizing attempts to remedy this, he carried the deformity throughout his life. Driven, perhaps because of the physical impediment, to be a very athletic man (he was a competent fencer as well as a powerful swimmer), Byron was often in pain because of the demands he placed upon his twisted appendage. Yet Polidori was a strange choice for a man with Byron's physical malady.

Known as a medical prodigy in his day, Polidori had not distinguished himself in the realm of orthopedics. Instead, Polidori's specialty was in the study of human blood. Given Byron's own interest in the legend of the vampire, one wonders why he needed a physician with this particular area of expertise. He was never known to have any ailment related to the blood.

There is further evidence from those close to him that Byron was tortured by some dark secret he hardly dared reveal. Byron's wife, just prior to their separation, attempted to make a case that Byron was insane. Among Annabella's chief complaints was his fascination with "certain Oriental legends" and the fact that he often associated himself with some kind of fallen spirit. She also accused him of drunkenness, adultery, and various threats against her person. There is little doubt that the Oriental legends she is referring to are those concerned with the vampire. A further detail she gives concerning his strange beliefs is that some ancient act of defiance had landed him in the flesh and caused him to labor subsequent lifetimes under some unnamed yet burdensome curse.

The rebel angel Lucifer was a popular archetype among the Romantic poets -- not as the source of universal evil, but rather as a kind of Biblical Prometheus. As one of the quintessential figures of the Romantic age, it is not surprising that Byron would have some fascination with Lucifer. Yet Byron seemed to extend the notion of his own nature beyond a symbolic diabolism to something stranger still. It was Byron's claim that he hurt all that he touched; his very embrace was poisonous. Sometimes, when Lady Byron went to comfort him, he would violently expel her from his chambers, swearing that he did this only for her own protection. When he grew foul tempered like this, he threatened that the harsh treatment was nothing compared to what he feared he *might* do to her.

In his darker moments, Byron would refuse to have his wife anywhere near him. He would berate himself, driving her off with claims that he was a murderer and worse. Lady Byron accepted this as merely a part of his delusion. As observed in his grandson's book *Astarte*, Byron himself would frequently pass off his belief in his more-than-human origins as a sort of joke he told to himself. And yet when pressed on the issue, Lady Byron reports that he would grow cunning, and lament that his soul had been "foredoomed to wickedness."

Notably, during the proceedings concerning their separation, Lady Byron also alleged that her husband had misused her in some "horrid" manner. When asked to elaborate on this, however, Lady Byron would never disclose the details about this particular abuse. She told Byron's friend Hobhouse that "nothing but the absolute necessity of justifying herself in court should wring [it] from her."

Hobhouse was determined to get the bottom of the matter. To this end, he presented Lady Byron with a list containing "every vice and sin, and crime, and horror in short of which a human being can be capable" so she could confirm or deny that the alleged abuse was there. Rape was included in the list, as was adultery, physical abuse, sodomy, incest and a variety of other perversions and wild pursuits. And yet all Lady Byron would say was that the alleged crime did not appear on Hobhouse's "black list." The matter was never clearly resolved, and it remained a topic of much speculation even after Byron's death.

Vampirism is one of the few things not included on Hobhouse's list. And yet it was as likely an evil for Byron to have committed as Satanism or piracy – both of which did appear on the famous black list. Perhaps Hobhouse felt this one thing was too far-fetched to include on the list – or perhaps he knew his friend too well and intentionally left it off so as not to incriminate him. Considering that the list contained every other evil that Byron had ever pretended to drunk or sober, serious or in jest, this omission is worthy of note. How likely is it that, Giaour-like, in a fit of passion, Byron drank his Lady's blood? She, half understanding the significance of this, was appropriately horrified – yet could never bring herself to even speak of it.

Byron, despite all his pretensions, was something of a religious man. His beliefs were touched by Calvanism early in his life, and so he had some strict perceptions of good and evil. He sometimes shrank from what he felt were his great sins, but accepted in a resigned way that he was inherently evil and couldn't fight this nature. He admitted to having married Lady Byron in the hopes that she would redeem him. She herself was a staunchly religious woman, and in his writing, Byron declared his hope that he could somehow ride to heaven by "hanging onto her hem."

It is clear that Byron felt different and alienated from those around him. Nowhere is this more eloquently expressed than in his play, *Manfred*. The title character, like so many of Byron's anti-heroes, is an obvious dramatization of Byron himself. Manfred is staunchly individualistic and unable to take comfort in the company of others, precisely like Byron himself. When troubled most, Manfred, like Byron, seeks out the majesty of nature to soothe his inner turmoil. Manfred has also partaken of a doomed relationship with his half-sister, a relationship which destroyed the woman in body and spirit. Although Byron's own half-sister Augusta did not die from her relationship with her younger brother, she was forever stained with the taint of their incest.

There are also implications in *Manfred* that the title character is more than human. At one point, he summons spirits from the ether, and they recognize him as a being like themselves. However, his nature is "clogged" in clay. To add further weight to Manfred's vampire-like qualities, he has a marked preference for the night, and he is also immortal. Admittedly, vampirism is not overtly stated in *Manfred* or any of the other autobiographical works, and yet a hint of it lingers through everything Byronic, like the scent of the grave clinging to a pale stranger's clothes.

There is one instance in Byron's life where vampiric passions seem clearly to come into play. Among his youthful seductions, Byron had a wild affair with Lady Caroline Lamb, a boyish waif with a penchant for dressing in men's clothes. While Byron's passions still waxed hot, he and Caro were inseparable, but once he tired of her, he grew distant and cruel. In one of her many desperate attempts to regain his affections, Caro sent Byron a gift of her hair. The enclosed letter includes references to exchanges of blood between the two of them, and the intriguing line: "I cut the hair too close & bled much more than you need..."

It is worth mentioning that Caroline, like Polidori, wrote a novel that caricatured Byron in print. The title character, Lord Glenarvon, is a cold-hearted and voracious lover who also dabbles in the black arts. Lamb's wicked Glenarvon very probably influenced Polidori's Ruthven, though Polidori painted his pseudo-Byron in a far more overtly vampiric guise.

Was there a basis for Polidori and Lamb's fictionalized image of Byron/ Ruthven the vampire? It could be argued that, given the belief system of the day, fiction would have been the only medium through which to expose some of Byron's more extraordinary beliefs and practices. Even so, because no direct material has been left by Byron himself on the matter, all theories on his factual connection to vampirism must remain mere speculation.

However, there are even a few post-mortem details that add a chilling conclusion to this exploration of Byron as a real-life vampire. In her biography of the poet, *The Life of Byron*, Elizabeth Longford includes a first-hand account of the opening of Byron's tomb in 1938 (114 years after his death). For anyone who is familiar with traditional vampire beliefs, Longford's description of this event is nothing short of amazing. Although she says nothing of vampires in her biography beyond a passing mention of the myth in connection to the poem, "The Giaour," Longford nevertheless makes an eloquent argument in favor of Byron's more-than-human nature in these last few observations:

After raising [the lid] we were able to see Lord Byron's body
Which was in an excellent state of preservation. No decomposition

> *had taken place and the head, torso and limbs were quite solid ... His sexual organ shewed quite abnormal development.*
>
> *Longford, 225-226*

The beginning of this narrative could well be the beginning of any number of famous vampire exhumations from the seventeenth and eighteenth centuries. The corpse showed no sign of decay and there is no stench noted by any of the observers. Longford's note on the state of Byron's genitals is intriguing as far as vampire cases are concerned: in many of the early exhumations, male vampires were often found to be in a state of pronounced tumescence (Paul Barber addresses potential reasons for this in his landmark work, *Vampires, Burial, and Death*). If this report were examined alongside the exhumations of earlier days, it would be hard to distinguish between Byron's corpse and the corpses of those individuals staked and beheaded as legitimate vampires.

One final note of interest: It was a common belief in the societies that spawned the Western vampire myth that certain individuals could exhibit vampiric tendencies during their natural lives. These highly feared *strigoi*, or living vampires, would of course transform into their more familiar undead counterparts once they were dead.

Blood-Drinkers in the Vampire Underground

2004 brought a great deal of exposure to the vampire community. It was the year that ***Mad, Mad House*** *aired, and it was the year that my own ground-breaking work,* ***The Psychic Vampire Codex*** *was published. One of the side effects of this new wide-spread exposure was that various authoritative agencies were seeking out experts on the vampire community to learn more about it. When a doctor associated with UCLA contacted me about a patient he was treating for a blood-borne disease who he had learned was also a practicing vampire, I immediately responded with as much information as I could muster on the issue of blood-drinking in the community. My notes and subsequent letters eventually developed into this article, slated for* ***Mysteries*** *magazine.*

Born in 1560, Countess Elizabeth Bathory was one of the historical prototypes of the vampire in modern fiction. Obsessed with her youth and beauty, Countess Bathory believed that she could preserve these things by bathing regularly in the blood of young maidens. In the course of her cruel and sadistic career, it is estimated that a grand total of 650 innocent village girls gave their lives to keep Elizabeth young and pretty. Often, girls from surrounding villages were rounded up by Elizabeth's servants and herded into her castle by the dozens. These hapless young things were often bound so tightly that when the first incision was made to bleed them into her bath, the blood would fountain out for several feet.

Bathory was ultimately brought to trial for her crimes. In 1611, she was tried and sentenced. According to the rules of the day, as a royal person, Bathory could not be executed for her actions. Instead, she was walled up in her own chambers and provided food and drink through a slot until such time as she naturally expired. By the time Bathory died in 1614, no one had seen her face or figure for many years, so it was impossible to tell if depriving her of her sanguine baths had also deprived her of her treasured youthful appearance.

Bathory was cousin to another Eastern European noble with a bloody appetite. Vlad III, prince and later ruler of Wallachia, distinguished himself as a bloodthirsty warlord who had a penchant for impaling people on long wooden stakes. In one famous incident, Vlad III is said to have dined among the dying who were erected around him in a forest of grisly stakes. It is believed that Vlad put 40,000 to 100,000 people to death in this fashion, earning him the nickname of "Tepes" – the Impaler.

We know Wallachia's Vlad III better by his other sobriquet: *Dracula.* Vlad's father was a knight in the Order of the Dragon, and as his child, Vlad III was known as "son of the dragon." In Romanian, "ula" means "son of" and "drac" is dragon. Conveniently enough for Vlad III's enemies, "drac" also means "devil" in Romanian, and to the many who found themselves on the wrong end of his stakes, he must have seemed the son of the Devil indeed.

Irishman Bram Stoker, stage manager of London's Lyceum Theater, probably learned of Tepes's brutal career through his friend, Hungarian scholar Arminius Vambery. The tales of Vlad's awful escapades so titillated Stoker, that the Transylvanian warlord became the primary source of inspiration for a character in a book Stoker was working on: *Dracula.* The book, and the character, are synonymous with the concept of vampires today.

Whether vampires of the undead variety actually exist may be a moot point. Certainly, none have stepped forward to reveal themselves today. Yet the archetype of the vampire is such a compelling one that an entire subculture has grown up around it and thrives America today.

With the vampire Don Henrie presiding over bloodbaths on SciFi's *Mad, Mad House* and the vampire subculture being featured on the *CSI: Vegas*, more and more people are asking about the truth behind the vampiric practice of drinking blood.

Blood is a touchy subject in the vampire subculture. A lot of groups who identify as vampires are really best described as psychic vampires – meaning they feed upon human vital energy. Most of these do not drink blood, and many even look down upon the practice of blood-drinking.

But it would be misleading to say that none of the people in the real vampire community drink blood. There are perhaps just as many self-identified vampires who sate their needs with human blood as there are vampires who feed purely upon energy. The blood-drinkers tend to be marginalized even within the vampire community because their practices are so controversial. However, they still exist, and there are probably more of them than most people think – or are comfortable admitting.

Within the vampire community, those who drink blood are commonly known as sanguines or sanguinarians. The word is taken from the Latin *sanguis*, which means literally, "blood."

A sanguine vampire – "sang vamp" for short – drinks blood from willing human donors on a semi-regular basis. This is admittedly a risky practice, and while there are several resources online that offer tips for making blood-drinking as safe as possible, such as Sanguinarius.org, a lot of the

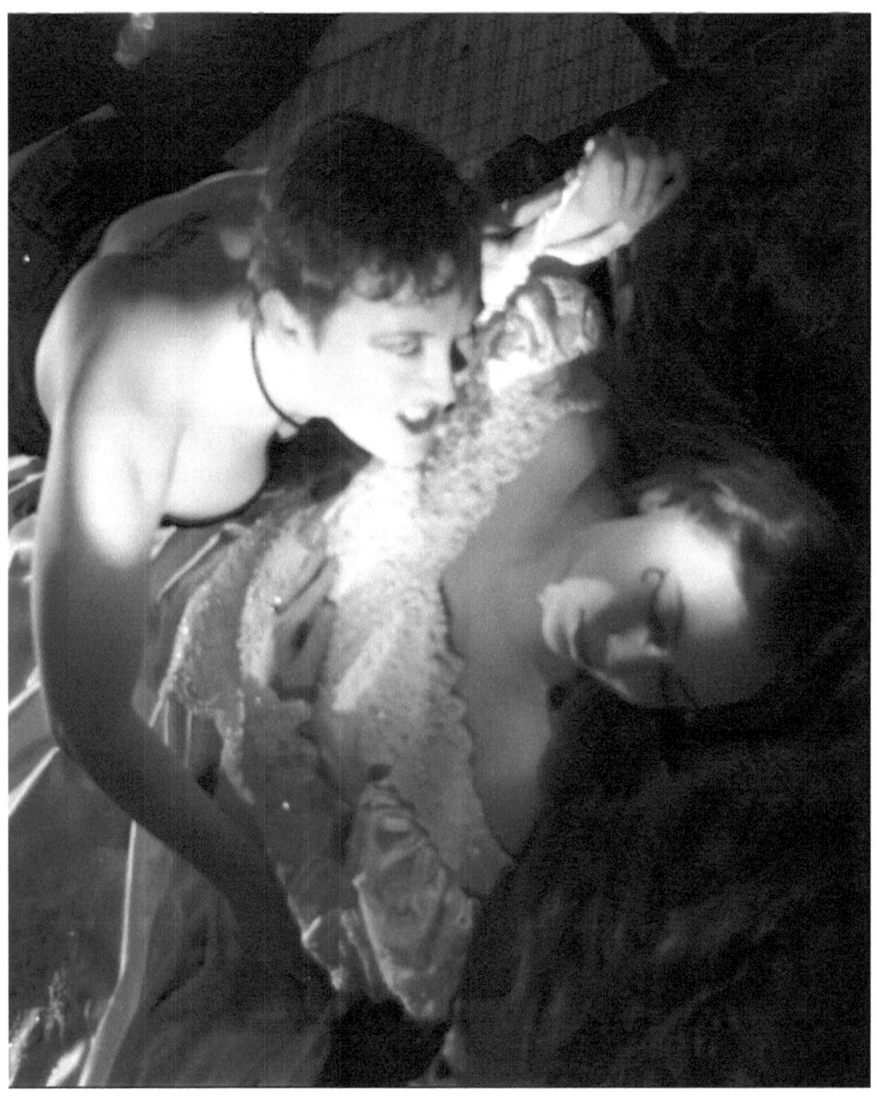

safety procedures rely heavily upon each individual's personal habits. Some people approach their blood-drinking as safely as possible. Others, unfortunately, are ignorant of their risks or simply do not care. Those with such lackadaisical attitudes endanger both themselves and their donors.

Issues of Safety

In the best case scenario, a responsible blood-drinker has him or herself tested regularly for blood-borne illness and sexually transmitted diseases (most notably AIDS and Hepatitis C). Such a responsible individual requires that any person who may serve as his or her donor also get such testing done and provide recent papers before any blood exchange begins. Because many vampires prefer to have more than one donor, this becomes especially important, as one person's illness can put several at risk.

Sadly, such a strict approach is not always followed. As this is a fringe practice, not all sanguines are as educated as they should be about blood-borne illnesses, nor are they as educated as they should be in how to minimize their risk of exposure. As this community's practices are a source of great controversy, honest and accurate educational resources are few and far between. No publisher will touch a book on blood vampirism, so at best, information can be found online or through underground networks of other blood-drinkers. Verifying the accuracy of such information can be difficult, especially for those who have no prior experience with vampirism and blood-borne disease.

Most sang vamps will at least ask about their prospective donor's sexual history, although individuals are often taken strictly at their word. A number of groups, such as House Eclipse (http://www.house-eclipse.org) in the DC area, require that their members get themselves tested and provide the paperwork that proves this at least once every six months. Involvement in such a group is not mandatory for blood-drinkers, however, so once again, the bottom line for safety rests upon each individual's personal choice.

Vampires and Donors

Because of health considerations and also because of the intimacy of feeding, a great many practicing vampires find a donor who also becomes their monogamous sexual partner. For the duration of the relationship, this person serves as the vampire's main source of blood. However, many others have at least two donors and sometimes three. Multiple donors are preferred by a number of sanguine vampires simply because this does not put the burden of providing blood on one person alone. Unlike the vampires of folklore or film, real vampires have no interest in killing the people who provide blood for them.

Getting even one donor is not always easy, even though there are people who willingly and happily offer themselves up for this role. Isolation and secrecy tend to make it difficult for many vampires to make contact with the people who would be willing to serve in this capacity.

Many of the big cities such as New York and Los Angeles have well-developed vampire undergrounds. In such cities, it is relatively easy to find the places where vampires and donors congregate. In less populated areas of the country, however, few such havens exist, and discovering their whereabouts can be very difficult to those who are just beginning to come out in the community. As a result, there are those who will take blood from any donor who comes along, jumping on an opportunity when it presents itself out of fear that it may be a long while before another chance appears. Despite the efforts of a number of leading figures in the community to discourage such blatantly risk-taking behavior, it nevertheless still persists.

Feeding Methodology

In addition to the risk simply inherit in the practice of imbibing human blood, there is of course the damage that can be incurred while taking it. Most sanguine vampires take great care to educate themselves in how to draw the blood they need while causing the least amount of pain and physical harm to their donor. Again, as information on these techniques is not exactly widespread, quite a few sang vamps have to experiment through trial and error before they find an ideal method.

Despite common misconceptions, sang vampires rarely if ever actually bite their donors in order to draw blood. Biting is exceptionally risky as there are all manner of potent bacteria living within the human mouth. In addition to the risk of infection, biting causes extensive bruising and other damage to the donor. Human teeth were simply not made to pierce flesh neatly and cleanly. Individuals known as fangsmiths exist within the subculture to provide sharp and prominent acrylic caps for people's canine teeth. These fake fangs could technically be used to draw blood, but the vast majority of sang vampires, if they wear fangs at all, prefer to wear them purely for show.

Typically, a blood-drinker with a mind toward safety uses sterilized lancets -- the sort sold at most drug stores for use by diabetics for testing their sugar levels. The lancets are individually packaged and come pre-sterilized. They are used once, then discarded. Some vampires will sterilize the area to be cut beforehand using rubbing alcohol or peroxide, though as they generally put this area into their mouth shortly after the cut has been made, this is not always strictly observed. Quite simply, sterilizing agent tends to leave a bad taste. The area is almost always rubbed down with alcohol or peroxide afterward and frequently covered with antibacterial gel such as neosporin.

The next cutting object of choice is a razor or exacto blade. These are recognized as risky devices -- one of the appeals of the lancet is the fact that it makes a cut of a pre-determined depth and it's pretty hard to have an accident with it. A razor is usually used to make shallow cuts along the insides of the arms, the upper arms, the upper thighs and sometimes the chest. Occasionally it's used to cut the tip of the finger. Once again, sometimes the area is sterilized beforehand, and sometimes it is not. This really depends on both the vampire and the donor and is ultimately a matter of personal choice. Once blood is drawn, the vampire sucks or licks it off and sterilizes the area after. Razors or other small blades are not always discarded after use, though typically efforts are made to sterilize them using alcohol, peroxide, and sometimes boiling.

In addition to lancets or razors, acupuncture needles are sometimes used. Performance artists Sky and Vlad of New York City employ needles like these in one of their blood-letting routines. To the accompaniment of drumming and other mood-altering music, Vlad is put into a trance. His partner, the petite lady Sky, then inserts a series of needles through the flesh of his forearm. Vlad uses the pain from this procedure to further launch his consciousness into a shamanic trance. The procedure has potent ritual and magickal qualities for Sky as well. When the needles are removed, she catches the resulting flow of blood in a metal bowl. As the ritual has united the two in magickal consciousness, Sky then uses the blood to paint an avatar of one of Vlad's past lives.

The blood drawn through this ritualistic method, which is vaguely reminiscent of Aztec blood-letting rites, is copious. As Sky and Vlad are both sanguine vampires in addition to magickal practitioners and performance artists, they have employed similar methods of withdrawing blood in their private feedings.

The Crimson Thirst

Considering the risks and social stigma, why do some people drink blood? The answer to this is complicated. Many sanguine vampires feel that they have a legitimate need to imbibe a small amount of human blood on a semi-regular basis in order to maintain their health and well-being. Admittedly, there is almost no medical evidence to support such claims. Several scholars have pointed out that a disease known as porphyria can cause sufferers to both react badly to sunlight and crave human blood. A severe iron deficiency is associated with porphyria, hence the blood-cravings. However, porphyria is an extremely rare disorder and the vast majority of self-professed sang-vamps do not suffer from it.

A number of sanguine vampires take a more metaphysical approach to their hunger, asserting that what they are really feeding upon is the lifeforce of their donors. For these, the blood serves only as a carrier or focus for the vital energy. The *omuli* of Zaire, the *varoyi* of Zimbabwe, and similar beings in folklore from around the world are born with just such a need. However, in our modern materialist culture, claims of such a spiritual hunger often seem more ludicrous than claims to a legitimate (albeit mysterious) medical need.

An argument could be made that at least some sanguine vampires have developed a psychological addiction to blood-drinking, and it is the symptoms of this addiction that they are experiencing when they feel the urge to feed. Others may simply be blood-fetishists who derive some kind of psycho-sexual release from the act of taking and drinking the blood.

The vampires themselves do not all agree on the source and nature of their need, and so it's impossible to really answer the question, "Why do vampires feed?" The fact remains, however, that a portion of the population experiences this sanguine hunger, and at some point, many of these will seek out a donor and feed.

Mirrors in Vampire Folklore

Since its introduction to the popular imagination, a number of traits have become indelibly linked with the vampire. Crosses, garlic, capes, and coffins have such potent associations that they have developed into vampiric clichés. Few of these qualities, however, were associated with the vampire in its beginnings in folklore and myth, instead growing out of the literary and cinematic traditions of the nineteenth and twentieth centuries. The following article, first written in 1996 for ***The Midnight Sun,*** *addresses the belief that vampires cast no reflection in mirrors.*

It has become a common belief that vampires cast no reflection. Supposedly the vampire, since he is a damned creature, has no soul and thus does not appear in mirrors. Yet this aspect of vampire mythology didn't even exist until Bram Stoker wrote *Dracula*. So where did he get it from?

There are a number of Eastern European superstitions that link mirrors with souls. For example, in Bulgaria, when the body of a deceased family member is displayed in a home, all the mirrors are covered or turned to the wall. It is believed that if the corpses' face is captured in the reflection of the mirror, he will bring death to another member of the family in a short while. A similar custom is observed during the Jewish period of mourning.

Mirrors are believed to reflect more than the physical visage: they are thought to capture something of the soul as well. Because of this, they can become thresholds onto the spirit world. The spirits of the dead can appear to the living through a mirror, and sometimes the spirit may even enter the realm of the living through the gateway created by a mirror.

Yet none of this has anything specifically to do with vampires, and if things had turned out just a little differently, our modern perception of vampires would not have anything to do with mirrors at all but with a painting. In his original writing of *Dracula*, Bram Stoker had Dracula commission an artist to paint his portrait. Stoker wanted to convey the idea that much of Dracula's appearance was subjective. It was a kind of glamour which he projected upon those around him. Stoker wanted the painter to try and capture Dracula as he appeared only to have the painting wind up looking like a centuries' old corpse.

This idea came from a conversation that occurred between Stoker, Hommy-Beg (a close friend of Stoker's who the novel *Dracula* is dedicated

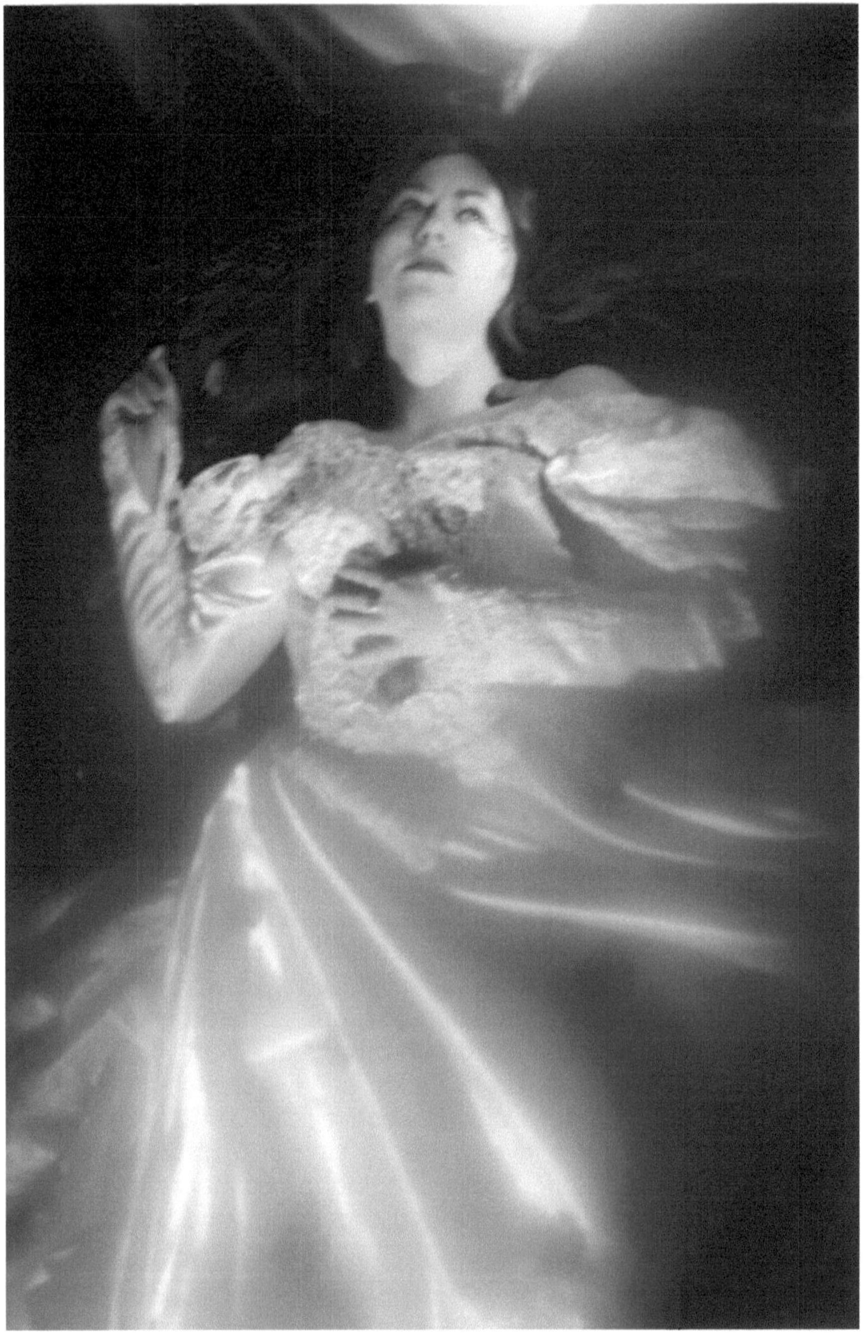

to), and the playwright Oscar Wilde. The three of them were discussing the actor Sir Henry Irving, a star of the theater in that day who Stoker happened to serve as manager for.

Irving, it seems, was renown for his stage presence. He was often described as having a mesmeric effect on the people around him. Stoker, in fact, when he heard Irving perform for the first time at a private reading, fell down in a dead swoon! Yet, despite how attractive he was in person and in character, Irving refused to have his picture taken. There was some speculation among the theater community in London that this was because most of Irving's allure could not actually be captured on film.

Stoker, Hommy-Beg, and Wilde were debating this at a dinner party (a party which, it might be mentioned, also included various high-ranking members of the Order of the Golden Dawn). The main question was whether subtle effects like a person's natural presence or "glamour" can adequately be captured in film or even on a canvas. The discussion got deeper, and they wondered if one could ever capture a person's soul in such a medium -- the soul being the truest measure of the man and therefore his most accurate likeness.

For Wilde, the fruits of this discussion was his short novel *The Picture of Dorian* Grey in which an artist does indeed successfully capture the likeness of a young man's soul in his painting. Once the soul and the likeness of Dorian are switched, young Dorian ceases to age, and all the effects of his debaucheries and wicked acts pile up not upon his living visage but upon the Dorian in the painting. For Stoker, the painting analogy did not work out as well, so he settled on having the infamous Count cast no reflection at all. The image was so powerful that more than a hundred years later, it remains alive and well.

Bram Stoker's Real Life Vampire

This article started life as a short in the International Society of Vampires newsletter, ***The Midnight Sun*** *back in 1996. When a number of readers expressed interest in the subject matter, I expanded the blurb into a full-fledged article for an issue of* ***Journal of the Dark.*** *Unfortunately,* ***JotD*** *folded before the full article could go to print. This is the first time the article in its entirety has been in print.*

Author Bram Stoker innovated on the vampire tale in ways that no writer has done before or since. There is something absolutely compelling about Stoker's work, such that despite many technical flaws within the novel, the story of Dracula remains fresh and alive in imaginations today.

Abraham Stoker was perhaps the last man in England anyone would have suspected of penning a supernatural thriller that would continue to titillate readers over a hundred years after its publication. Born into solid, middle-class Irish stock, Stoker was a practical man better known among his friends for his physical prowess than his literary aspirations. Many mainstream writers have wondered what caused the staid, middle-class Irishman who managed London's Lyceum Theater to turn his pen to so strange a topic as vampires. It is tempting for vampire lovers to suppose that Stoker had an encounter with a vampire in real life. As whimsical as this notion sounds, it may not be far from the truth.

When you know that something like psychic vampirism exists, it's tempting to speculate about who is and who isn't a psychic vampire. Mostly this is just an amusing intellectual exercise -- after all, there's no real way to prove conclusively whether or not someone from history was actually a psychic vampire. But there are a few historical figures who really stand out as possibilities. Ironically enough, one of these served as the inspiration for Stoker's famous *Dracula.*

Stoker was the manager of London's Lyceum Theater. Through his position at the theater, Stoker worked with famed Shakespearean actor, Sir Henry Irving. A tall, gaunt man with intense eyes and an arresting presence, Irving was a legend in London. Stoker and others believed that Irving had a "mesmeric" personality and could affect people's energies from across a room. In fact, when Stoker first attended a reading by Irving, Stoker attracted Irving's attention from the stage, presumably because the actor intended to impress his future stage manager. Irving focused most of the dramatic reading toward Stoker with such intensity that Stoker felt overwhelmed by the actor's personality. He was so overcome by Irving's presence that Stoker fell down in a swoon.

It should come as no surprise that Stoker patterned at least some of the character of Dracula off of Sir Henry Irving. A little-known fact about the novel *Dracula* is that Stoker originally intended it to be a stage play, and he wanted none other than Henry Irving to fill the title role. Irving himself felt the story was trash and had no trouble telling Stoker so. He refused to bring Dracula to life on the stage – perhaps because some of the Count's darker traits hit a little too close to home. Whatever the real reason Irving turned down the role, it left Stoker crushed, and while he went on to publish *Dracula* as a novel, relations between the author and the actor were never quite the same again.

Did Irving object to the role of Dracula because he felt the work lacked merit or did he have deeper reasons for wanting to dissociate himself from Stoker's Count? Count Dracula is depicted as having been a tyrant in his earlier days, and Irving was renown for being overbearing. Often Stoker commented that he felt overwhelmed by the actor, and in some cases he even felt preyed upon by him. Certainly he felt that Irving held some kind of undue sway over him, but whenever Stoker worked up the nerve to confront Irving on his overbearing behavior, the moment he got into Irving's presence all the fight went out of him and he became his loyal toady once more. The ambivalent relationship that Stoker had with his actor is reflected in two semi-autobiographical characters who appear in Dracula. The first character is rather obvious, as he happens to share Stoker's first name. Abraham Van Helsing is the powerful, self-assured figure Stoker wished he could be in relation to Irving, a man who had the ability to save himself and others from the wiles of the Count.

Considering that Irving had a reputation for being hard on actresses, it's little wonder that Stoker wished he could be Van Helsing and protect the ladies in his care from that actor's "monstrous" side. However, as previously noted, Stoker was rarely able to directly stand up to Sir Irving, and he despised this weakness in himself. The precise level of self-loathing that this weakness inspired becomes evident when we consider that the other character that is believed to reflect Stoker in the novel is none other than the pitiful, obsequious Renfield.

There can be little doubt that Stoker was drawing from real-life experiences for some of his inspiration for *Dracula*. Although the actual events of the story are obviously fictitious, the psychological undercurrents at work in the novel, especially in the relations between Renfield, Van Helsing, and

Dracula, were at work in Stoker's own life. But this still doesn't make a clear case for Henry Irving's identity as a real-life vampire. Beyond the fact that Irving could be intense and over-bearing, why would a prosaic middle-class Irishman like Stoker make the leap of attributing vampiric qualities to the actor he managed?

Inevitably, we must return to Stoker's first real experience of Sir Henry Irving, the dramatic reading that left Stoker in a senseless heap upon the floor. Enough ink had bee spilled over Irving's mesmeric abilities to manipulate crowds that is would be safe to assume that Stoker himself believed that there was something beyond the pale in Irving's affect on him. This in itself still might not be enough to imply "vampire" if not for the fact that Stoker was actively involved with a number of individuals in London society who not only believed in the existence of psychic vampires, but some of them even wrote on how to protect oneself from their attacks – attacks that sounded suspiciously like the effect Irving had upon Stoker.

The Hermetic Order of the Golden Dawn was an occult society founded in 1888 and run out of the Isis-Urania Temple in London. At the time of its founding, the Golden Dawn attracted many of the city's literati and social elite. It boasted among its membership the actresses Florence Farr and Annie Horniman, Irish poet W.B. Yeats, and Constance Wilde -- wife to the famous Irish poet and playwright, Oscar Wilde.

The Golden Dawn was dedicated to the study of magick, and members spent their time researching and compiling a great deal of esoteric information from ancient texts and Medieval grimoires. In fact, it is through the efforts of Golden Dawn founder S.L. MacGregor Matthews that several of these grimoires still circulate in publication today.

The members of the Golden Dawn felt that there was some truth to historic beliefs in the supernatural, but that the truth had gotten confused over time with superstition and folklore. Some of their efforts went to sifting through myth, folklore, and superstition in order to find the lost grains of truth. Among their areas of concern were traditional supernatural creatures, including demons, spirits, and vampires. In the instructional texts of the Golden Dawn, called "Flying Rolls," there appear at least two instances where psychic vampirism is addressed, and methods of protecting oneself from it are described.

It is interesting to note how many of the members of this secret mystical organization Stoker came into contact with in his daily life. Constance Wilde was well-known to Stoker through her husband Oscar. Stoker and Wilde had gone to school together and even competed for the attentions of the same woman. Many of the actresses and other theater people involved in the Golden Dawn worked with Stoker directly through the Lyceum Theater, and Stoker's wife Florence hosted regular social events in her London home which included many of these members of the Golden Dawn.

Despite the strict oath of secrecy that was sworn by all members of the Golden Dawn not to discuss the issues of the order with those outside the order, it is hard to imagine that the animated dinner conversations between the literary friends did not at least occasionally stray to topics of the occult and esoteric. And Stoker was there, perhaps adding some opinions of his own but definitely taking it all in.

Significant to the argument that Stoker's work was somehow influenced by the Golden Dawn and its beliefs is the simple fact that Stoker published Dracula in 1897 but had been working on developing the story for almost a decade prior to its publication. The first notes biographers can distinctly link to the creation of Dracula are then contemporaneous with the early days of the Golden Dawn shortly before and immediately after its founding. Once again, how much of the occult and esoteric was discussed between these scholars, actors, and writers prior to their forming an organized group devoted to such topics is open to debate.

It is known that on at least one occasion, the conversation at Mrs. Stoker's social event waxed toward things metaphysical. In a now-famous conversation, Stoker, Wilde, and their mutual friend Hommy-Beg, were discussing the properties of the human soul in relation to being photographed or otherwise captured in art. The discussion inspired Stoker to have Count Dracula cast no reflection, as a sign of his lack of a human soul. Wilde went on to write the chilling tale of a young man whose vices and sins are reflected not on his own form but on the image of his portrait. Significantly, the individual who inspired this fertile line of conversation was none other than Sir Henry Irving -- whose dislike of being photographed was renown throughout London.

Did Stoker even mention the effect that Irving had upon him to any of his Golden Dawn cronies? The fact that he discussed at least one of Irving's quirks with that circle of friends suggests that this is a very strong possibility. Did Stoker himself believe that Sir Henry Irving was a vampire? He certainly fit the classic description of a predatory psychic vampire as it appears in the works of the Golden Dawn. Does this mean that Irving was in fact a real life vampire? There's no way to really know, but every time another reader picks up the novel *Dracula* and shudders at the commingled repulsion and attraction they feel for the title character, they are in part experiencing Stoker's own relationship with his tumultuous actor.

Vampirism and the Darkside

Written originally for ***kheperu.org*** *in 2001, this article, like many others, has been reprinted on a number of vampire and Pagan sites online. Both the folkloric and literary traditions depict vampires as antinomian beings, damned by their very existence, and this sense of inherent darkness often bleeds over into the identities of people who have adopted the vampire as a personal archetype. This article addresses that notion, dispelling common misconceptions about darkness and its relationship with things most people traditionally identify as "evil".*

Most of us are aware that many Pagans and Wiccans consider vampirism to be something akin to black magick. This is to say nothing of the Christians who, if they accept our validity at all, seem to be under the impression that we must be demonic or Satanic in origin. I'm not going to try to defend our kind to the Christians. They've got their own problems, mainly the notion that no one has the 411 on God except them, and until they sort their general intolerance out, I don't think there's much of a chance of having a positive dialogue with them. But a lot of us in the vampire community are Pagan or Wiccan, or we work directly with people of those faiths. And so it's important for us to understand why they object to us, and why they are wrong in that objection.

As mentioned previously, the main tenet of the Wiccan/Pagan faith is "An it harm none, do what thou wilt." Some groups will add "in word, thought, or deed" to the "An it harm none" part. The very act of feeding upon another person is immediately construed as causing harm. If nothing physical is done to the "victim," then the harm is in the very thought, the act of directing one's magickal will toward the purpose of taking something vital away from another. This is seen as a selfish act, and as such falls into the realm of what the Wiccans consider black magick. A lot of what vampires do naturally, because it largely involves manipulating, influencing, or affecting others, can at the very least be considered grey, and grey is a very hazy area of magick and morality for the Wiccan and Pagan communities.

Now, it would be a fallacy for me to try and say that vampirism is not dark. There is a very clear and present element of darkness in who we are and what we do. Most of us are attracted toward dark images and symbols; we resonate with dark gods and goddesses (if we resonate with deities at all); we all tend to wear dark clothing and we shun the bright, day-lit hours.

The mistake the Pagans and Wiccans make in their attitude toward vampirism is not in perceiving it as dark, but in perceiving the darkness as necessarily evil and destructive.

I think having an awareness of our "dark side" or shadow, if you want to use the Jungian term, is one of the things which typifies us vampires. Many Pagans and Wiccans tend to embrace the light exclusively, rejecting the darkness just as thoroughly as most Christians do. This ultimately overbalances the religion, making it blind to one full half of existence and experience. For good or for bad, there is darkness in all of us, and that darkness needs to be accepted and understood for a person to be whole.

Being a vampire, there is a certain amount of darkness that I cannot ignore. It is a part of me, something that I am reminded of on a constant basis. I feel a greater surge of power with the nightfall. This surge of power extends to the Wheel of the Year so that on holidays like Samhain and the Winter Solstice, both darkside holidays, my power is at its peak. Many of my strengths and abilities come from a potentially negative drive to feed upon the life force of those around me. I am attracted toward wearing dark clothing, not only because I like Gothic fashions, but also because I feel more comfortable and "at home" in dark colors. It's significant to note that darker colors tend to absorb more energy, and energy absorption is very in tune with who and what I am on a fundamental level.

There is just no denying it: Darkness is a part of us, and in many ways, it is what defines us as what we are. Yet where many Pagans, Wiccans, Christians, and others will embrace the light to the exclusion of all things dark, I've noticed that most vampires do not make the same mistake where darkness is concerned. Certainly we embrace the dark side of our natures, and yet we have no problem balancing our darkness with the light. Many of us are healers. Many of us make certain that we feed responsibly, honing our skills so the exchange is reciprocal for those who offer life to us. We are not beings bent on destructive or malevolent actions. Instead, we appreciate the balance of darkness and light, for we feel this balance very keenly within ourselves every day and night of our lives.

It is my opinion that vampires are a viable and necessary part of the modern magickal community, especially *because* we represent a dynamic and ultimately positive facet of darkness. Being a vampire is not just about feeding upon life. That is what we do, but not necessarily what we are. It is our place to represent darkness in a world blinded by the light. We are about being different and accepting that difference as something that ultimately empowers us and makes us unique. We are about accepting the dark within ourselves as well as the light and embracing both of these qualities in order to make ourselves whole beings. We are about celebrating the

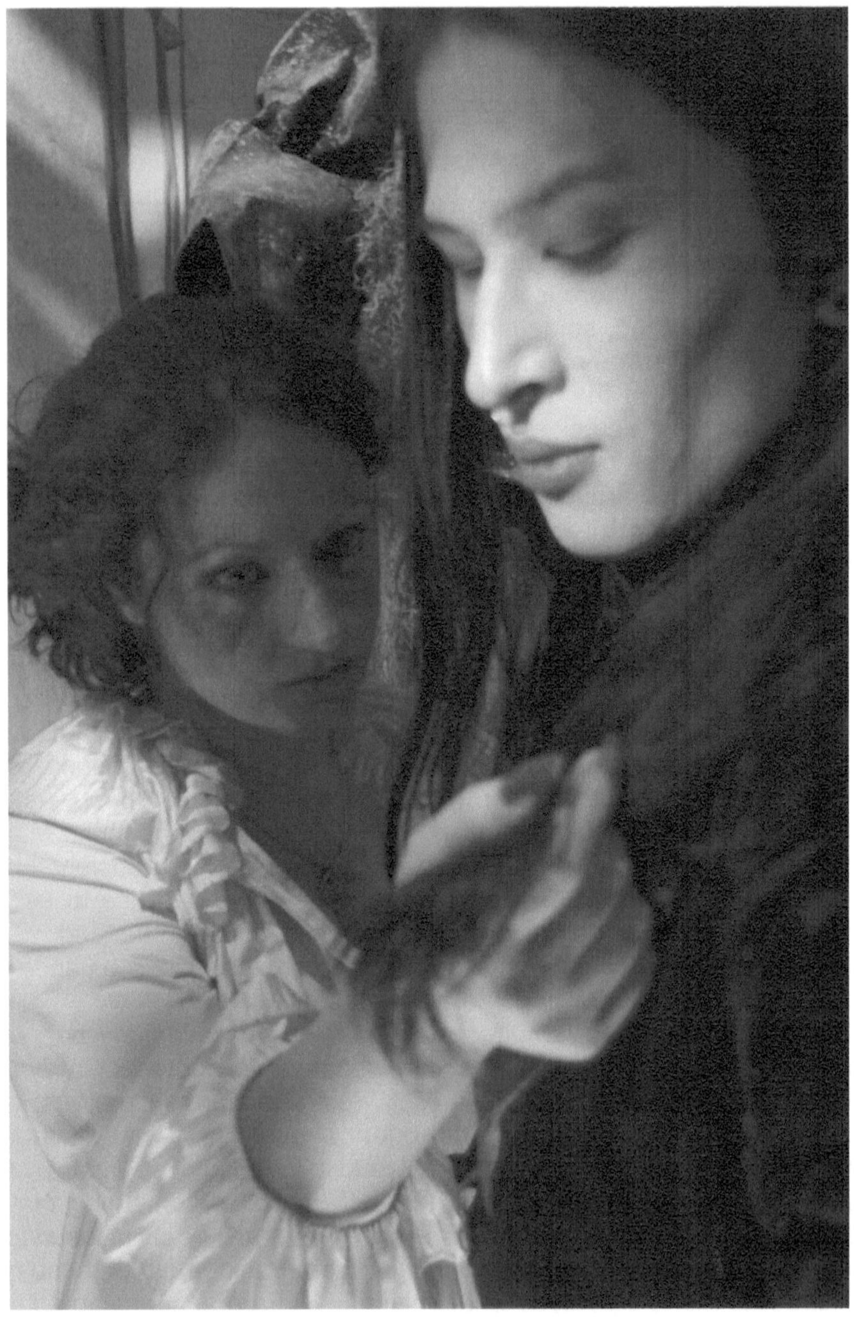

thresholds: body and spirit, pleasure and pain, death and life.

Our lives should be lived as a message to the world about the beauty of accepting the whole self, of acknowledging our darkness and making peace with it, of living without guilt and without shame, and celebrating the unique and beautiful essence of every single soul.

VAMPIRES AND SUNLIGHT

When I was interviewed in the fall of 2000 for a vampire documentary scheduled to air on Britain's XYTV, one of the things I was asked to explain was the issue modern vampires often have with sunlight. Although folkloric vampires are clearly "children of the night," the notion that sunlight incinerates vampires is actually rooted in twentieth century cinema, most notably in Murnau's ***Nosferatu****. The conversation that ensued was later developed into this article, which was then published to* **kheperu.org.**

It's straight out of every cheesy vampire movie you've ever seen: the vampire gets up, walks out into a room flooded with light, and if he doesn't burst into flames, at the very least he winces and puts on a pair of sunglasses. It's an inescapable stereotype: vampires can't stand bright light. Now, it is of course silly to presume that real vampires, when exposed to sunlight, will go up in flames and be reduced to ash. As far as I'm aware, that belief was created entirely by Hollywood and has no basis in vampire folklore whatsoever. Stoker had Dracula running around London during the day – he just made it clear that Dracula's powers were weakened when the sun was up. Most of the vampires in folklore need the help of a good, roaring pyre to be reduced to ash, although folklorically speaking most of the old myths agree that vampires prefer the night for their predations and can rarely be caught out of their coffins after sunrise.

But that's the undead – the myth that has grown up over the ages. Folklore might have a grain of truth to it, but most of it is just nonsense, right? After all, real vampires sleep in beds just like ordinary folk, and it should follow that real, living vampires shouldn't have too much trouble walking around at noon. But there is the uncomfortable reality that sunlight has some kind of effect on us that most of us cannot explain.

I wrestled with this one for quite a while. I tried to convince myself that it was all just in my head and all those uncomfortable physical reactions I was having were purely psychosomatic delusions. I even valiantly tried swearing off my sunglasses on a family trip to Arizona. But it didn't take much of the brutal desert sun to convince me that, psychosomatic or not, I still had trouble seeing unless I had something to shade my eyes. And that's to say nothing of the headache, nausea, and distressingly rapid sunburn.

But then someone made an off-hand observation about sunlight and energy and suddenly it all made sense. The answer was so simple and so obvious that I was amazed that it hadn't occurred to me before. Sunlight is radiation. It's not just visible light. It's heat and ultraviolet rays and a whole lot of other things we can't properly see all pounding down on us. Because of our metaphysical natures, we who describe ourselves as vampires are highly sensitive to all forms of energy. We react and interact with it in strange and often intense ways. How many of us have walked by a television or radio only to have the reception fuzz out in our presence? When we move, whatever disturbance we were causing with the radio waves settles down and the reception clears up again. How many of us have accidentally blown out lightbulbs or other electrical appliances with our mere presence? Digital cameras, cellphone batteries, even car batteries can have a hard time holding a charge if we spend too much time in close proximity to them. So why *wouldn't* we have an unusual reaction to sunlight as well?

It's so basic. Sunlight is energy. Metaphysically speaking, it's solar *chi*. Now, plants are probably the organisms that are best equipped to process solar *chi*, but most people like feeling the sun warming them as well. It's healthy for them to get a few rays once in a while, and recent studies on the body's interaction with sunlight, particularly in relation to a naturally-produced substance called melatonin, show that regular exposure to sunlight helps to regulate peoples' sleeping schedules.

Vampires seem to function on a different set of rules than the majority of other people. On some fundamental level, the way we react to many things is a bit different from the norm, starting with our relationship with vital energy and possibly extending to our relationship with *all* forms of energy. Although we're as human as everyone else physically, something about our spiritual natures makes it almost impossible to process solar *chi* in any kind of positive fashion. It's too much.

It's too *something*, because nearly every vampire I have ever spoken with has had about the same complaints regarding sunlight: It hurts their eyes. Prolonged exposure makes them dizzy, nauseous, and weak. The warmth of the sun on their skin does not feel pleasant; it feels prickly, uncomfortable and very, very hot. They burn very easily and in the end have all the symptoms of heat exhaustion or sunstroke after only ten or fifteen minutes outside. Sometimes the reactions are more severe, sometimes they're a bit more bearable, but generally speaking, modern vampires get sick in the sun.

Sunlight is radiation, and it's a radiation that can be harmful to everyone, vampire or not. These days, with the ozone layer being depleted so rapidly, the rays that come through to us are even more unhealthy. Sunlight is getting to be too much even for ordinary people to bear, as can be evidenced by the rising numbers of cases of skin cancer each year. Most ordinary people still don't feel anything negative in the sunlight streaming down on them, but that's because they're divorced from their subtle senses in ways that vampires, by nature, cannot be. When we go out into direct sunlight, our bodies are telling us something. Messages like that are not idle ones. Sunlight, or at least some parts of it, is harmful. We're hypersensitive to that harm. We just have to accept that and learn to live with it.

Vampires in Faerie Lore

*I first encountered the notion of vampiric faeries in Brian Froud and Alan Lee's lush and imaginative art book, **Faeries**. I explored the connection of these otherworldly beings with vampires in an essay on Christina Rosetti's poem **Goblin Market** in 1994 and in several short pieces that ran in both **Shadowdance** and **The Midnight Sun** between 1992 and 1995. In 1996, this research was expanded into the following article which ran in a later issue of **The Midnight Sun**.*

The faeries of the British Isles are rarely the harmless, wispy little sprites we have come to associate with the term "fairy." Strange, outlandish, grotesque and macabre, they are alien beings who exist in a realm removed from that of the living. Immortal, ageless, and timeless, the fey share a number of characteristics with the undead.

Like the vampires of folklore, faeries are most active during in-between times such as dusk and pre-dawn. They are also quite active at night, and in some traditions, direct sunlight even causes them discomfort and harm. Holy symbols can ward them away, and it is believed that they cannot set foot on hallowed ground. Like vampires, faeries are sometimes shapeshifters, although they rarely appear as wolves. In Dartmoor, pixies can take the form of hedgehogs, and according to folktales from Cornwall, they may take the form of ants.

The realm of Faerie is a realm of eternal twilight, timeless and preternaturally beautiful. Sometimes known as the Summerlands, mortals can occasionally enter this realm through underground passages which open up in wild places or underneath huge, earthen mounds known as faerie raths.

Because it is a realm out of time where none age and grow old and because most of its entrances lie underground, the realm of Faerie has sometimes been equated with the realm of the dead. This connection between the faeries and the dead is reinforced by the fact that the places traditionally known to be faerie raths are actually the sites of ancient burials. The Hosting of the Sidhe, a great gathering of the fey, is most likely to occur on Samhain, when the spirits of the dead are also believed to walk among the living.

The connection between faeries and the undead seems particularly clear when we look at the Leanan-sidhe of Ireland. Her name means "the fairy girl-friend," and on the Isle of Man, she is considered to be something

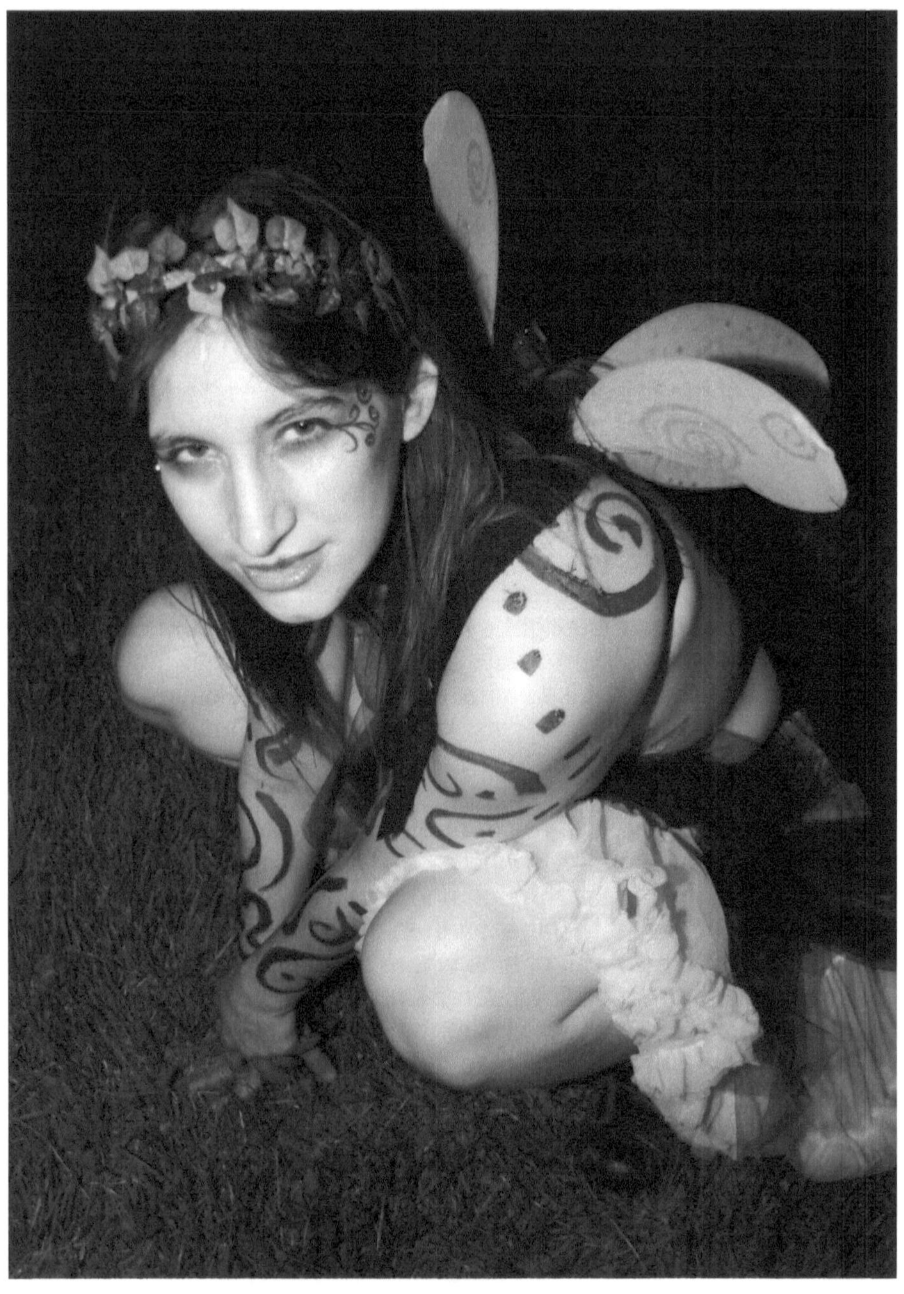

of a muse of poetry. She appears to young men as a beautiful woman. In this form, she seduces them and drinks their blood, appearing to them again and again over the course of many months. The young men who fall under her spell find themselves inspired by creativity. Their minds burn brilliantly like a star, and then wink out, all their light and vitality spent in her deadly arms.

The Tao of Vampirism

This is another good article that started its life on the House Kheperu e-list. As a student of comparative religions, I make it a point to scour the belief systems of others in order to find cognates of my own beliefs. I've always been driven by the notion that if we stripped away the culturally and temporally specific language and symbol-systems, all the magick, metaphysics, and mysticism of the world would look the same. Even so, there are times when I am pleasantly shocked to find that we all have more in common than we dream.

I've long been fascinated by Taoism and its related energy techniques, mainly because so many of the texts I've read correlate with the nature and function of vital energy as I've learned of it through personal experience. However, only some texts are translated into English, and not all of the translations are good. Additionally, with the coming of Communism and the Cultural Revolution, much of this material has been suppressed in China itself. So it's very hard here in the States to find good resources and good teachers for Taoist material, especially Taoist alchemy, which is a completely different animal from the philosophical Taoism most Westerners are familiar with.

My life being punctuated by meaningful coincidences, I found myself at a job in 2002 that opened some significant doors on this very line of inquiry. I applied to work night audit at a hotel, partly in the hopes that the long, lonely nights would afford me time to write. As it turned out, the hotel I was hired by is owned by Chinese immigrants. The general manager is also Chinese and happens to have graduated from the same college that I did. When I met him, I was struck by his energy. He had that feel to him of someone regularly meditates and works with energy. I figured he was a Taoist, but wasn't quite sure how to approach him on the matter.

A few weeks into the job, he solved the problem for me. One afternoon, when I was working second shift, he came up to me at the desk and just stared very calmly at me for a few moments. It was a frank and open stare, and I knew enough about his culture at that point to suspect that he was trying to frame a question for me. After a few moments, he asked point-blank, "You work with energy, alchemy, right?"

At this point, I was somehow used to the notion that I could tell by feel alone if others worked with energy but I was still adjusting to the notion that someone could get the same intuitive feeling off of me. Mutely, I just nodded, wondering what other surprises my manager would have up his sleeve.

"You know the elixir, the 'pill,' when you circulate that, how does it work for you?"

I blinked slowly, understanding that what he was referring to was precisely the aspect of applied Taoism alchemy that I had been trying to find written material on. It was the aspect of Taoism that had to do with the cultivation of spiritual — and in some cases physical — immortality, and here was my general manager, asking me pointed questions about its most advanced techniques. Needless to say, we had a pretty mind-blowing conversation, and by the end of it, I had had a question that has bothered me about Taoism for years now neatly answered.

It has to do with what we in the West call vampirism.

You see, most of the Taoist texts that I've read talk about meditation and gathering *chi,* or vital energy. And they give you lots of breathing exercises for the first stage of meditation. And they tell you that the next stage is about gathering your *chi*, then concentrating it, then circulating it around. There is some hazy material on exactly where one gets this *chi,* and it is tantalizingly implied that sometimes more advanced practitioners have to actively take it from somewhere. That taking is what Western metaphysicians call vampirism, but the wording was always just hazy enough to leave me doubting whether or not the process that I call "feeding" is what they were really alluding to.

Now, I've always been afraid to jump to conclusions on this matter simply because I am certainly biased and could be reading too much into the text. It doesn't help that most texts refer to certain techniques by flowery and traditional names, like "Abstention from Grain" or "Circuit of the Golden Flower." I know that these are literal translations in English of something that is without a doubt deeply metaphoric in the original Chinese. But without any explanation for what these obviously symbolic phrases actually mean, it's like shooting in the dark sometimes.

And yet, despite all of that, here is my general manager comparing notes with me about meditation and energy work. We're talking shop, trying to work around some gaps in language to see whether or not we do things the same way. And then he comes out with this bit of wisdom: "The next stage is gathering *chi*, and most people think this is just your own *chi* to be gathered. But it is not just your own -- you must take *chi* from outside of you, from other sources."

Bingo! I think, as he goes on explicitly to describe the process I have come to know as "feeding."

A lot of people who call themselves vampires still think that this is a bad thing. They draw energy from nature, from the elements, from animals, from storms — and of course, from people — all the while feeling half guilty about it and assuming that there is something broken in them that causes this need. But according to Taoism -- not just the texts, but now from a living practitioner -- this is not "vampirism" with all the negative connotations we in the West have learned to associate with it. The need to take in energy from the world around you is a necessary and natural part of cultivating spirit.

As Ling continued to explain it, the more one works with vital energy, cultivating and refining it, the more abilities one can harness that use this energy. In *Opening the Dragon Gate,* translated by Thomas Cleary, Taoist wizards are said to be able to melt snow high atop mountains with nothing more than their body heat, heal entire villages of pressing maladies, and even levitate. But all of these abilities must be fueled by something. The natural fuel is of course the energy that one cultivates in order to place their talents within reach.

There is something to the psychic part of "psychic vampire." Nearly everyone I know who identifies with this term is also empathic, if not telepathic, has exhibited some level of psychokinetic ability, at least on the unconscious level of interfering with electrical appliances, and practices techniques that many would identify as magick. Psychic vampires are doing something with energy nearly every day. So, if you look at it from Ling's perspective, vampirism is *natural.* It's how individuals who have cultivated spirit and who operate on a heightened level interact with their world.

So why do we in this culture get so bent out of shape in accepting this in ourselves? Why are we so tortured by the notion that vampirism must be some kind of curse, or a disease?

Our culture has no precedent for the notion of energy, let alone the notion of energy exchange. Thus, when we sense these things, when we feel the need to "gather chi from outside sources," we wonder what's wrong with us. Even having this drive is enough to make most of us question our sanity, as such thing as an invisible vital force isn't supposed to exist.

But the problem is not with us. The problem is with the assumptions we've been raised on. Western culture has put all of its focus on the material world to the exclusion of anything spiritual. Thus, those of us for whom the spiritual side is an obvious, integral, and undeniable part of our existence, that awareness itself seems like some kind of terrible handicap. Think about living in a world of blind people where being able to see is so unusual that it's seen as a curse! You don't need to imagine it -- we're living in that world right now.

Community versus Egoism

A good friend and fellow author got thrown head-first into the intricacies of the vampire community one eventful October weekend in 2002. An avowed agnostic and materialist, he didn't exactly see eye-to-eye with all our beliefs. And yet, the issue that gave him the most trouble, and which he addresses in his fictionalization of that weekend, ***Pedestrian Wolves,*** *is this question: why would individuals who define themselves as vampires seek to build a community? He felt that the identity of the vampire and the activity of community-building were mutually exclusive concepts. Some days, I think he's right. On other days, I write articles like this.*

As we have seen elsewhere in this book, there are two very real historical figures who, if lifted from their lives a hundred and two hundred years ago, would fit quite naturally into the modern vampire community. In many ways, the lives of these two men shaped the modern image of the vampire, and the literary legacy surrounding both of them helped build the foundations of our modern subculture. These two men are Lord Byron, who was turned by John William Polidori into the vampire Lord Ruthven, and Sir Henry Irving, the actor whom Bram Stoker cast in his mind to play his famous Count Dracula.

Byron and Irving, though they held great fascination for those drawn to them, also repulsed those closest to them with the self-same power from which that fascination arose.

One has only to read Stoker's letter and journals to see the mixed feelings he had for Irving, and of course there's a complex psychological drama inherent in casting oneself as both Renfield and Van Helsing. Where Irving was concerned, Stoker loved him and loathed him -- and loathed himself for loving him.

And it was always the same with Byron, though he, more than Irving, showed an awareness of what he wrought upon those closest to him. He couldn't help but attract others, for he had the bright and terrible beauty of a falling star. But even he knew that those who touched by his fire were invariably wrecked.

Such individuals do not a community make -- and it is just as well, for what a community that would be! There is enough wrangling and melodrama and back-biting in the vampire community as it stands in this modern age. Could you imagine someone like Byron at the heart of a vampire

Household? A man at once arrogant and self-loathing, wishing to be noble yet ruled by his passions all the same?

Perhaps it was a good thing that two of his former lovers, Polidori and Lady Caroline Lamb, sought to warn the world of him in their books. (Lamb's story, which was the first appearance of Lord Ruthven, is entitled *Glenarvon* and is much harder to find than Polidori's novella, *The Vampyre*).

But these two people highlight the problems inherent in any community made up of vampires: there's a truth that we often hate to admit to ourselves, and that is the fact that in order to act upon our natures, we must fall prey to a certain level of selfishness. We must learn to put ourselves first, at least in some things.

How else could one ever justify taking the life force from another being? Certainly, it can be done in as positive a manner as possible. With care and discipline it does not have to hurt, and it even can help -- but in the end, what you are taking, you know is vital to you -- and so it must be vital to those people that you take it from. You know that you suffer without it, and of course they, your victims or your donors, must suffer if too frequently fed upon.

And yet we do it. We come to a point where we can justify the temporary loss of another so that we ourselves may feel well. Thus, on some deep, instinctive level, we will always be inherently selfish beings.

This does not lend itself well to the building of a community. Most vampires that I know are stiff-necked and obdurate people, unflinchingly individualistic, with a refusal to bend to any will save their own.

This is where you get the inherent fear of authority that is so prevalent in the scene -- no one wants to acknowledge leaders because everyone wants to lead. We rail against systems and organizations, elders and hierophants because, when it comes down to it, our natural inclination is to be our own first and last authority.

So rather than asking why there was no community in the past, perhaps it will be more revealing to ask, why do we have community now? How is it that such a mass of out-spoken individualists can learn -- or even want -- to work together?

And I think the answer comes down to something anyone engaged in a metaphysical community ultimately strives for: self-knowledge.

In this day and age, we have the luxury of self-knowledge. Byron suspected something about himself, but with no information readily at hand, he spent his whole life doubting his nature. He never achieved that moment of self-acceptance that liberates us to then analyze the whole Self.

Since he never could solidly admit what he was, how could he ever hope to explore it?

And Irving -- Irving shows even less self-awareness of his nature, although the more I read about the man, the more I'm inclined to suggest that he knew, but didn't care. He was what he was, and it suited him. He felt no need to further explore it, define it, or bring it under any sort of rule. It worked for him on the stage, had all the ladies of London panting after his Macbeths and his Hamlets, and that was all that really mattered to the man whose stage manager penned *Dracula*.

But here in this age -- at least within our subculture, what we are is accepted. Vampirism is known to exist, and while the dominant culture still resists our reality, thanks to the dialogue between the metaphysical beliefs of the East and the West, the mechanics of our condition are reasonably well understood. So once we recognize this quality within ourselves and accept that we are vampiric -- then we can begin to explore how we wish to express that in our lives.

We have the luxury of not being slaves to our passions, because information exists to show us another way. We do not have to live in self-denial, repressing our needs until they surface in some manner that we cannot control. We can gaze within and accept our natures, and we can learn to be at peace with what we are. When one functions purely on instinct, there is no hope of applying right and wrong to actions. But once you have attained full knowledge of what drives you -- at that point you can make educated decisions to act or not act.

And these choices, to not be overwhelmed by our hunger, not to be devoured by our egoism and selfishness -- these allow us to recognize the benefits inherent in a community. We can choose to get along despite our differences, because -- if nothing else -- exposure to other people like us helps to put our own experiences into perspective. Self-knowledge allows us to work around our flaws and build a community, and the building of that community generates even greater self-knowledge.

Perhaps it's simply the ultimate expression of selfishness: by helping others, we only help ourselves.

And the beauty of it is that, by helping those around us -- working with them rather than lording ourselves over them or preying upon them -- we actually benefit more than if we were to look out strictly for our own well-being.

Dealing with the V-word

*There was a time when we overhauled the **www.kheperu.org** site and tried removing as many of the overt references to vampirism as possible. I, and a number of other people in the community, had gotten tired of trying to defend our association with that word. There was a lot of good writing on the Kheperu site that was getting glossed over and ignored just because readers couldn't read past "vampire." The new, improved and more socially acceptable version of the site didn't last. First of all, it felt like we were covering things up like guilty children caught doing something naughty under the blankets. Secondly, there was just no way to accurately put a word to a fundamental part of our energy work without recourse to "vampirism." When we once again redesigned the site, I wrote an early version of this article, part manifesto, part apology.*

V*ampire.* There are days when I hate that word. Don't get me wrong - it has its uses. But I hate the impression that the V-word invariably gives people who are outside of our community. It's a label, and a convenient way to judge us without ever bothering to understand our practices and our beliefs.

One friend who I had known for many years, got a link to my site, took one look at the v-word there, and has not spoken to me since - neither did she read any of the content beyond that one word. Prior to that, I had been a role-model she had looked up to and expressed deep respect for. Afterward, I can only imagine what she thinks.

In early 2004, upon purchasing a house and moving into a quiet cul-de-sac community, one neighbor got hold of the address for my author site online. Upon seeing who I was and what I wrote about, she had her husband go to the police to see whether or not I was "dangerous." Ultimately, a police report was filed simply because I'd *moved in next door to her.* She said she didn't feel safe, and thought the community needed to be warned about people like me. A little rag of a local paper carried the story with the exaggerated headline of *Vampire Evades Arrest* and consequently we had a city councilman going door to door in the community, letting people know about the vampire who'd moved in. Fortunately most of the neighbors realized we were not living in the Dark Ages, unlike the McCarthyian councilman and the paranoid housewife. Several even made a point to come over and get to know me. But all the drama started just because of the v-word and its inevitable connection to me.

It's fair to say that I've wrestled with that seven-lettered word nearly all of my life. Certainly, like a vampire, I feed upon the vital life force of others to maintain my own well-being. And yet I do not stalk around in a cape, transform into a bat, or sleep in a coffin. I am immortal in spirit only, and though I seem to age more slowly than others, I have no doubt that this body will eventually grow old and die. But then there's my aversion to sunlight and the exceptional photosensitivity of my eyes. I do prefer night-time, and work third shift as a result. And even though I love Renaissance festivals and amusements parks (rollercoasters are my favorite), I have to limit those activities because being out all day in the sun is just going to make me sick.

There was a time when I strongly identified with the word because it was the first thing I'd run across that explained what I was. But, over time, my enthusiasm waned, because, though it fit, it was also dead-wrong. Like so many people in the vampire community, I continued to use the word, altering the definition at least to myself. But this only confused matters more because when I said "vampire", I'd mean one thing, but those who were listening just thought "Lestat".

Thanks to 19th century literature and 20th century film, "vampire" is such a loaded word. It was a loaded word twenty years ago, when I'd hit upon it to describe myself, and since then it's been shaped by Anne Rice, role-playing and Buffy fanatics. Vampires have become something of the darling of pop culture, and while this has at least increased peoples' interest in what's really out there, it has also saturated them with images that have nothing to do with what real vampires live every day.

I often wonder if there's any way to combat this. While I respect those individuals who prefer to keep their vampirism private, I personally would like to be able to admit what I am without having people scoff or look at me in fear. My vampirism is a part of me, and if people can't accept my vampirism, then really, they can't accept who I am.

For a while, my answer was to get away from the v-word. I stripped it from my website. I tried to find new words of describing the same thing. But the only thing this taught me is you can't escape the truth.

First, the absence of the word resulted in confusion for a lot of the real vampires who were searching the site for answers on what they were. Then there were the countless Pagans, Wiccans, New Agers and others who visited the site, read through its material, and occasionally wrote me asking, "You realize what you're describing is called psychic vampirism, don't you?"

And if I had any pretensions after that of escaping the v-word, there was the fact that simply walking down the street or visiting the mall, I'd be stared at by children and often by parents. And, no matter how casual or normally I was dressed, I could hear the whispers behind me. The sweet little four-year-old at the museum cinched it -- "Look at the vampire, Mommy!" -- and me in dress pants and a gray button-down shirt! Out of the mouths of babes, indeed.

In the end, I had to approach the word like an ill-fitting suit. It wasn't the classiest suit on the rack and the cuffs were a little too short. But yet, of all the other clothes offered, it was still the closest fit.

Given the option of wearing that suit, or no suit at all -- the choice was clear. I'd seen worse suits.

So ... *I'm a vampire.*

Sure, it's a stereotype and a nice, convenient box. Sure, some people are going to stare and look askance. But really, when it comes down to it: if they can't see beyond the limits of that one little word, are they really trying to accept me for me?

Vampires ... In Their Own Words

This collection of letters was originally included in an early version of the ***Psychic Vampire Codex*** *manuscript. This version of the manuscript, prepared at the same time that the* ***Vampyre Codex*** *was first being circulated by itself throughout the 'net, was intended to introduce the concept of our community to a more general audience. In 1999, I was not certain if the time was right to attempt publishing such a work outside of the vampire community, and so I kept the manuscript on my hard drive, adding to it, taking elements away, and generally revising things until I arrived at the version that finally made its way to Red Wheel/Weiser in late 2003.*

Over the years, I have maintained a massive correspondence with vampires all over the globe. Mostly, we have written to one another in order to share experiences and obtain a sense of community. Correspondence between vampires is often very guarded at first. It is hard to know whether the person on the other end is legitimate or not. Although there is a great impulse to share who and what we are with others who understand, too many of us know from direct experience what it is like to reveal too much, and be judged, or to confide profound personal details to someone who turns out to be a poser – someone who's only pretending to be a vampire for their personal amusement.

Usually those who are pretending to vampirism eventually reveal themselves by making outrageous claims. They will claim to be many hundreds or many thousands of years old. They will lay claim to the powers and weaknesses one only encounters in movies and books. They fixate on blood and bloodlust, and often even claim to have killed people in order to sate their hunger.

These people are pretty easy to differentiate from the real vampires. Real vampires very rarely make wild, unsubstantiated claims. They are usually very cautious about claiming any "supernatural" ability, and they demonstrate skepticism on their own part as well as a rational approach to the more extraordinary aspects of their natures. There are some aspects of vampirism that you really have to experience in order to understand, like how it feels to feed from another person or what the memories of past lives are really like. Knowledge of these things, tentatively revealed at first, usually helps correspondents establish one another's legitimacy, and then a profound and mutually self-revelatory relationship can ensue.

Once I have gained the trust and friendship of my correspondents, they are very forthcoming. We all love sharing our experiences, primarily to see if anyone else has had the same thing happen to them. As it has been mentioned again and again, it is easy to doubt your sanity when the extraordinary experiences are yours alone. When you learn that other people who could not possibly know about these secret things have experienced them too, you don't feel like so much of a freak. Even if you live in an isolated area of the country, surrounded by conservative people who would do you bodily harm if you ever revealed half of your personal beliefs to them, you suddenly feel much less alone. The sense of community, however tenuous and wide-spread, is a comfort.

You will see several different themes often repeated in the letters which follow. One of the primary themes is the sense of isolation and the desire for community. Almost all of us have grown up knowing that we were different, but never daring to hope that others were different just like us. The very act of corresponding is one of the first steps of reaching out to others like ourselves and accepting that we are not the only ones.

Another main thing accomplished through the correspondence is an exchange of experiences. This goes along with the sense of isolation. All our lives, there have been these other aspects to our perceptions and experiences that no one else around us seemed to share. Experiences which for us occur on an everyday basis are at best accepted only by fringe members of the mainstream community. As a result, few of us ever find anyone in our local communities whom we can confide in. Although we are bursting with experiences that we'd like to share in order to get a different perspective, most people would look upon us as freaks or worse if we ever opened up about these things in a mundane setting.

And so we struggle to find others like ourselves who have lived the same kind of lives and had the same kind of experiences so we can finally talk about them to someone who understands. This exchange is also vital to our sense of community, and it helps us to establish what it really means to be what we are. By comparing and contrasting ideas, beliefs, perceptions, and experiences, we find out what is normal for people like us, what is a little unusual, and what seems truly unique to ourselves alone.

Finally, we discuss personal spirituality. This is pretty much how we interpret our unique experiences and put them into context within our lives. I have found that it is nearly impossible to live as we do, so aware of both the material and the spiritual aspect of existence, and not develop some kind of spirituality. Think about it. Your very existence is defined by your ability to sense and manipulate the energy of other people. You are acutely aware of your own energy and subtle body. The entire realm of the subtle reality is something you experience hand in hand with ordinary reality every day. If you are going to believe in yourself and not convince yourself that you're crazy, then you have to believe that there is more to the world than just the physical, material existence. It's as simple as that.

Although they are spiritual, very few vampires are religious. Most vampires see religion and spirituality as two distinctly different things. Religion is equated with dogma and, by extension, with a lack of individual freedom in terms of belief. Consider that most major world religions generally seek to translate mystical experience into something that can be quantified, defined, and reduced to one particular set of rules. There is little flexibility in these rules, and the diversity of individual experience is almost always stifled. Spirituality, on the other hand, is an intensely individual thing. Spirituality is developed from direct, personal experience of the divine, unmediated by scripture or dogma. Thus, as far as most vampires are concerned, spirituality is the liberated ideal of what religion profess to strive toward but fail to achieve because of the fetters of dogma.

Most vampires may have started out in an organized religion, but their very nature conflicts with the teachings of most accepted world religions. It is impossible to keep the faith of a religion which views you as inherently wrong, if not outright evil. A great many vampires have been attracted to Wicca and neo-Paganism as a result, but even these religions are a little too dogmatized for our kind. Wicca, with its creed of "An it harm none" is seen by many as being antithetical to vampirism, and many Wiccans are openly hostile toward vampires. And so vampires find themselves defining their own spirituality which fits neither here not there but which is defined by each individual to suit his or her own needs.

And now, the letters. The first letter in this series is from a vampire in Athens, Greece who I made contact with only a few years ago. He is very articulate and intelligent, and his English is nearly flawless. This is the second or third letter we've exchanged. At the writing of this letter, I had already told him a little about myself and my group. This is his response. It is a pretty typical piece of vampire mail.

Athens 25/11/98

I was glad to read that [your group] are psychic vampires and not "blood sucking" humans like most "vampires" around. So my first question is how did you realise your nature and at what age? Were there any signs of your vampiric identity when you were still a child? Has anyone in your family vampiric tendencies? About myself, others in my family had metaphysical experiences, but none can store their energy or take from others. The only exception is my grandma though she isn't conscious at all of vampirism. Yet she has unveiled many vampiric truths and sometimes surprises me for that. I don't know if the Bloodline is passed genetically to others, but I suspect so, judging from the fact that those humans to which I've shown the way and practices of vampirism never make it.

--Nikos

The following is an out-take from a letter written in late 1996. The writer is a man in his thirties who lived in central Pennsylvania. In the second paragraph, he talks about making the transition from mortal to vampire in a previous life. In an earlier letter, we had already established that he believed vampires had undergone a ritual or process which allowed them to separate themselves from their physical bodies and therefore escape the wheel of death and rebirth. Vampires, in his system, can best be described as astral entities who, if they take up mortal flesh at all, do so under their own compunction and on their own terms. I've since fallen out of contact with this gentleman -- quite regrettably. It is my sincere hope that he does not mind my sharing this, with his anonymity in tact, for the sake of sharing knowledge with others.

21 November 1996

So you've come across two more of our kind and possibly a third -- good. I agree with your statement concerning the responsibilities that come with the knowledge of our true nature. It is easy for a person to call themselves by some name in a feeble attempt to belong to the ideal of the name. To know, to understand and to be requires much more. However, for those of us who are well aware (unclouded??) of our nature, it is no chore. Our instincts grow stronger with our awareness and as you have pointed out -- grow weaker with ignorance. I do not refer to ignorance as a lack of intelligence of mental functionality, but rather as one, who for whatever reasons, chooses to ignore that which they know to be true.

The "Potentials" as you call them. I can see some as simply being so engrossed with "playing the part" of a human that, after a time, they forget what is the play and what is real. We are the ulti-

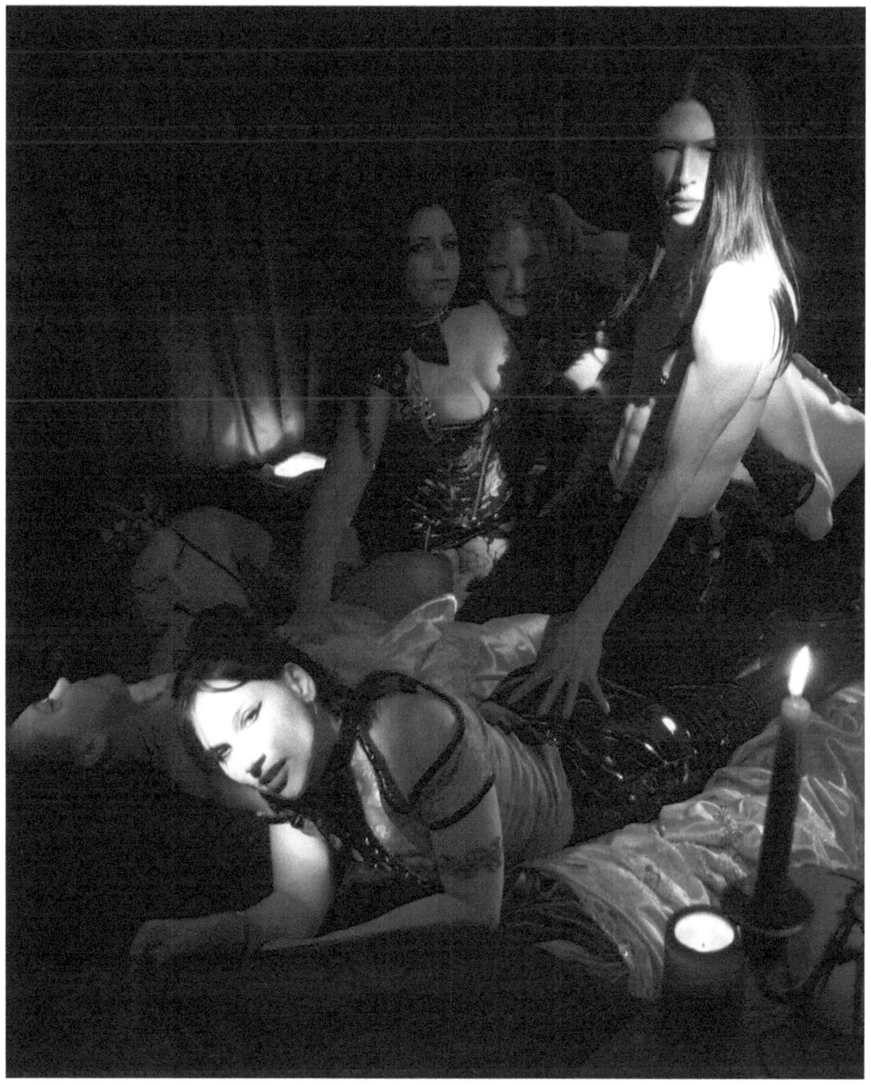

mate chameleons after all. We can fit in anywhere we choose as anything we wish. It allows us to get close to those who we wish to feed off. A more complicated form of stalking than simply wearing camouflage (UV and scent clear) and quietly sneaking up on something. Some of the best feeding requires direct interaction with the host, where the host is willingly (if unknowingly) giving us what we need. It is an acquired talent.

As to your question about the ridiculous references in literature about being "made into" a Vampire, I have to agree with you. You are born to this life, freely chosen and accepted. I will go so far as to say their (sic) is ample possibility for a new Vampire to be born, but present science and economics have distracted many of those who could possibly make the transition. I can remember back to the time before I left my mortality behind and the transition itself (as well as the pain). I can remember discussion with others, who made the transition with me, as to the ramifications of our actions. Endless debates over the differing viewpoints of morality. Discussions of insanity, delusional mentality, and other psychosis. It seems like those discussions will never end, and perhaps that is wise. As long as we know what we are, how we are, and keep in mind why we are, then I see no reason why any of those discussions should worry us.

As to my experiences with awaking the knowledge in others -- I must admit I haven't encountered any "Potentials" in this life, but have in others. In those instances where I have, simple manipulation (mind games) has always brought about their remembering and return. I have never had to reveal anything which would put me (in whatever body I then existed) in danger (and we do remember those times!). And I must also admit that there has (sic) been times where I deliberately did not awaken an individual simply because of the risk involved.

--Eloran, PA

As I've said many times before, it is not an easy thing to be a vampire in this day and age. Again and again in the letters I receive, I hear from other vampires around the world how they are mistreated and discriminated against because of what they are. Because the mundane world is so oppressive to us, most of our kind hide in the shadows, keeping their true natures secret from their neighbors and co-workers and essentially leading a double life.

Some of us have tried to "come out"-- and we have been slapped down for it. One sanguine vamp that I know appeared on the Ricki Lake Show in 1996 after being interviewed in Jeff Guinn's *Something in the Blood*. She is still feeling the repercussions of coming out about her vampirism so publicly. In a letter dated January 24, 1999, she shares some of her woes with me. Although what she has gone through has been extreme, she is hardly an isolated case among us.

> *I have finally found an employer who doesn't care about my life or what the guests in our hotel say about me. Becoming a freak-show on international television has its consequences ... It is the ignorance of the daylight world that continuously pushes me (or at least tries) into the ground. However, I will not disappear. I will not stay quiet. The vampire community is real. We are poets, doctors, lawyers, artists, teachers -- we are all the things that the daylight world is. For the most part (there are a few loose cannons), we hurt no one. For those of us who are born this way it has thus far been a hard existence. It should not have to be that way. I have risked everything to speak out about who I am and that I should have the same rights as everyone else.*
>
> *--DarkRose, FL*
> *letter postmarked 1999*

In recent years, my vampire contacts have not been limited to pen pals with whom I exchanged physical letters. The Internet has provided a fertile place for vampire communities to take seed and grow. In the earliest days of my correspondence, I had to rely on small-press publications which were advertised largely by adswaps and word-of-mouth to make any contact at all with other vampires.

Such little fanzines and newsletters were not only hard to find, they were hard to maintain (I ran one myself). They were never self-sustaining ventures but financed purely by their editors as a labor of love. The Internet, which is largely free and accessible to practically everyone, has seen a recent upsurgence in vampire-related groups. Many of these are for role-players or the kind of posers that real vampires tend to avoid, but an increasing number of message boards, newsgroups, websites, and elists are attracting a very serious, intelligent, and well-informed community of real vampires. What follows is a typical first-contact email with a vampire who, like myself, was pleasantly surprised to find another rational, intelligent soul in the Internet:

12/13/99 e-mail

As for the term, "vampire", I do agree. It's often referred to indirectly or as the "v" word since none of us are particularly fond of it. Words that substitute it are often "family", "hardcore feeders" or "nephilim". An open dialogue would be interesting. What do you consider to be defining characteristics of yourself and others? Set beliefs and theories in regards to vampirism? I am unsure where to begin for myself.

--Dae, CA

As the years go on, what will continue to build and define the vampire community is our communication with one another. As we share our experiences and ideas through the medium of the written word, on e-lists, through websites, or blogging tools like LiveJournal, we forge ties among one another, networking and building common ground. And as time goes on, I think the personal sharing will be reinforced more and more by individuals within our community who write articles, books and stories based on their beliefs; people who create music, art and even theater that is inspired by what we experience everyday. And in this manner, we will nurture the community until it becomes a culture in its own right, something which we all have participated in, and which, through its expression of our identity as vampires, will support and enrich us all.

Vampires in Myth and Folklore

The following section is a mini vampire encyclopedia. I was asked to write it for the second ***Vampyre Almanac*** *in 1999, and it has become such a standard in the community that most people recopy its entries without even realizing who the original author was. I am indebted to both Matthew Bunson of* ***The Vampire Encyclopedia*** *and Rob Brautigam of www.shroudeater.com (formerly* ***International Vampire****) for information regarding many of these folkloric entities.*

Adze: An African vampire native to parts of Ghana and Togo. The *adze* is a tribal sorcerer who has gained special powers from a spirit which he has allowed to possess him. The *adze* drinks not only blood but also palm oil and the milk from coconuts. Like many vampires, it prefers to prey upon children, seeking out the best-looking ones above all. When it goes about feeding, the *adze* takes the form of a firefly, but if it is captured, it will revert to human form.

Algul: An Arabian entity, mentioned particularly in the *1001 Nights*, who feasts upon the flesh of the dead. In the Arabian tradition, this creature is usually female and she eats the bodies of dead infants as well as that of older dead. This being gave rise to our modern concept of the ghoul, which is usually thought to be a corpse itself which rises from the dead, but which, in fact according to the folklore, is a living person driven to feed upon the dead.

Alp: A German creature whose name shares the same root as "elf." The *alp* is active at night, flying forth invisibly to visit sleepers in their beds. They suck blood from men or infants, and like many Romanian vampires, they are also known to suck the milk of women and cattle. The *alp* is believed to wear a special cap to make itself invisible. In addition to this, it is a shape-shifter, capable assuming the form of a cat, bird, pig, or dog.

Aluka: There is a passage in Proverbs 30:14-16, which describes vampire-like entities. They are described as a group "whose incisors are like swords, whose teeth are like knives," who feed upon the needy and the poor and who suck blood like the leech. The leech mentioned is the horse-leech, which gave rise to the notion of a vampire or blood-sucking demon known in Latin as the *sanguisuga*. The *aluka* may be related to the Arabian *algul*, a beautiful woman with a hunger for human flesh.

Aniukha: This Mongolian vampire is the spirit of a shaman who has used his powers to return from the dead. All shaman have returned from the dead once: a ritual death and rebirth is part of their initiation into becoming a shaman. However, even though the shaman exists on the threshold between life and death, he is expected to use the powers this grants him only for the good of his community. When he uses these powers for his own ends, he can become a fearsome being indeed. Once a shaman has become an *aniukha*, the best way to dispose of him is to drive an aspen stake through his corpse and then cremate him.

Aptrgongumenn: A being from Norse legend whose name means "walking dead." The *aptrgongumenn* was an unfortunate soul whose body was called up from the grave, usually by a powerful necromancer. The necromancer then forced the risen corpse to do his bidding. Binding runes were often placed on gravestones in order to prevent the dead from walking, whether through the intervention of magick, or through their own ill-fate.

Astral Vampire: A kind of predatory spirit described in the teachings of the Golden Dawn and later in the writings of occultist Dion Fortune. Generally speaking, an astral vampire is a being which feeds off the energy of others. Astral vampires can be wholly non-physical entities, existing purely in the subtle reality. They may also be living, physical beings who have the ability to move and interact on the subtle realm. Most traditional magickal and occult systems (Wicca, neo-Paganism, etc.,) tend to view astral vampires as malevolent and predatory. This kind of reputation is overblown and somewhat undeserved. Although an astral vampire attack can be an inconvenience, it is in no way life-threatening. Most victims of an astral vampire attack don't even realize anything has been taken from them. Those who have an awareness of their subtle, energy body will feel at the most lethargic and a bit headachy. Astral vampire attacks are quite rare. Few astral or psychic vampires attack unwilling victims. Most seem to prefer achieving a symbiotic relationship with one or more willing participants who provide energy with full knowledge of the long-term effects.

Aswang Mananangal: A shape-shifting vampire from the Philippines, the *aswang* is often a respectable member of the community by day. During the night, however, the *aswang* detaches its head from its body and flies about, searching for prey. Seeing an *aswang* at night is a gruesome sight, for not only are they flying, bodiless heads, but their entrails are still attached at the throat and trail wetly behind them. *Aswang* are also often accompanied by small birds that help them locate their prey. *Aswang* feed upon human flesh and blood, internal organs, and mucus. Like many vampiric entities, they prefer to feed upon infants and children.

Bajang: A Malaysian vampire, often kept by sorcerers and used much like a *polong*. Appearing most often as wild cat, the *bajang* has a fondness for attacking children. *Bajang* are dangerous spirits because they can be captured by certain sorcerers and used against their enemies. Captured *bajang* are kept in a special bamboo vessel known as a *tabong* and fed upon milk and eggs. If an imprisoned *bajang* is not kept sufficiently fed, it will turn upon his owner. If a *bajang* is successfully kept and cared for, it can be passed down for generations, rather like a spiritual heirloom.

How do you get your own *bajang*? Stand over the grave of a stillborn child and call out its spirit with the proper spells and incantations. This spirit will become a *bajang* which explains why, out of jealousy for their lives, a roaming *bajang* will often attack infants and small children.

Baobhan-sith: A Scottish faerie with vampiric qualities. Like the Irish *leanan-sidhe*, the *baobhan-sith* is a beautiful maiden who seduces young men. Clad in a long gown of faerie green, she will appear to young men and join them in dance and song. There is a malicious magick to her music, however. Although her partners will not realize it, something in her voice and her touch draws their very blood up through their pores. In this way, she feeds on their life. The next morning, their corpses will be found where she has left them, completely drained of blood.

Bebarlangs: An interesting tribe of people native to the Philippines. The *berbalangs* are believed to have the ability to send their souls forth from their bodies and, in this form, prey upon their neighbors. In this spirit form, the *bebarlangs* are efficient vampires, feeding upon the life-force and vitality of their victims until those victims sicken and die. *Bebarlangs* are living people and it is unclear whether this ability to vampirize others is a natural trait or learned skill.

Bhuta: An Indian creature, the *bhuta* appears as a flickering light which hovers above the ground. Much like European will o' the wisps, these lights haunts forests and waste places. Unlike will o' the wisps, however, which are only seen at night, the unfortunate traveler in India may encounter a *bhuta* during the day as well as the night. *Bhuta* are often demonic spirits which were never human at all, but sometimes a *bhuta* is created when a human suffers a violent or untimely death. *Bhuta* feed upon human flesh, although since they fly about in the air and never land, all one has to do is lie stretched out upon the ground beneath them to avoid their deadly touch. They most often attack people who do not show a proper respect to the dead. *Bhuta* are not only believed to be able to enter a person's body and make them sicken and die, they are also blamed for storms, bad crops, freak accidents, and any illness which plagues livestock.

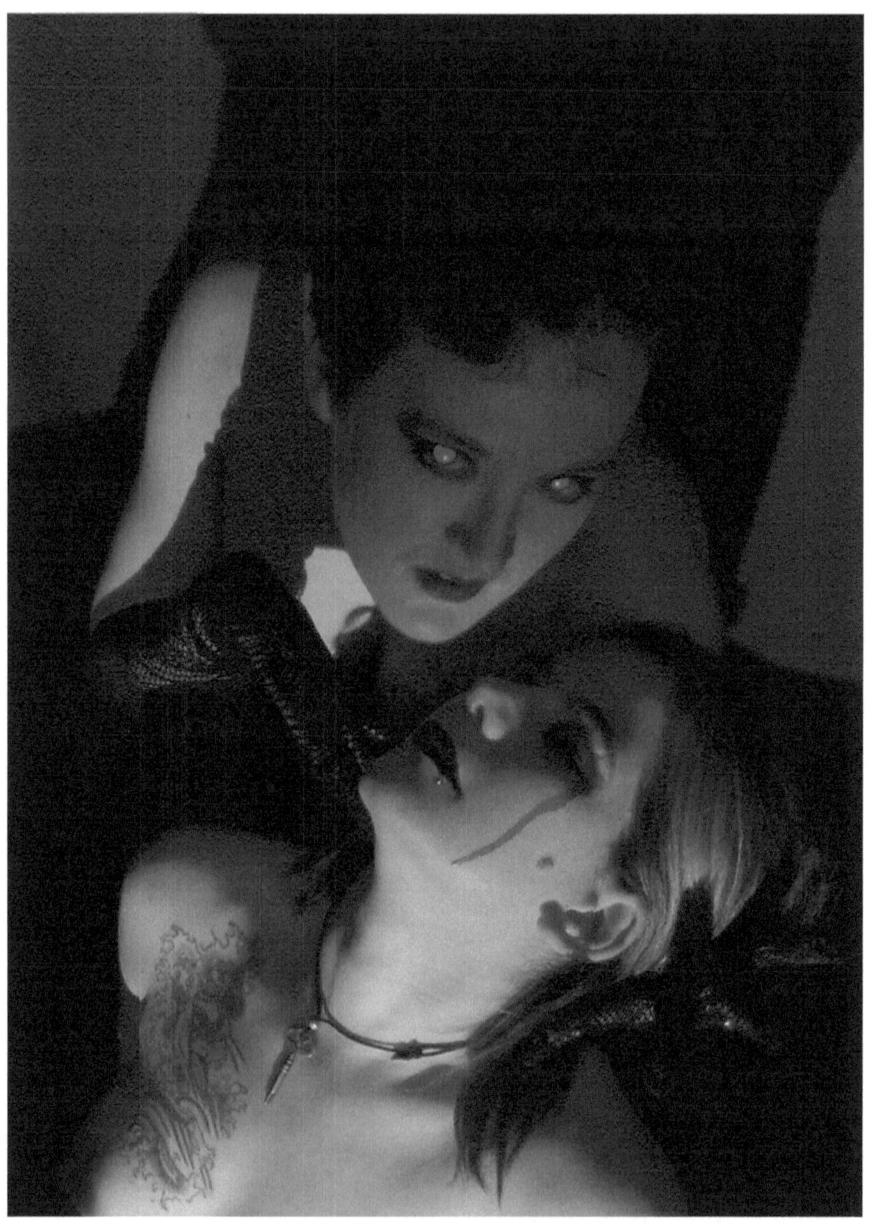

Blood: In the Biblical Book of Leviticus, the Israelites are told that if they are going to eat of the flesh of an animal, they must first kill the animal and let its blood spill out upon the ground. It is very important that the Israelites do not eat the blood with the flesh, for the blood of the animal is equated with its life (*nephesh*). The Hebrew word used here may also be translated as "breath" or "spirit." Thus, the passage is saying that the Israelites cannot feed upon the spirit of an animal, only its flesh.

Most of our modern vampire traditions can be traced to Eastern Europe. At the time that the folkloric tradition was being developed, Eastern Europe was Christian. Very devoutly Christian. Every time they attended Mass, the Christians gathered to drink the blood of Christ. This was a powerful and mysterious ritual to them, with many psychological ramifications. The Book of Leviticus clearly stated: *The blood is the life.* Thus, when these Eastern European villagers reported that vampires were stealing away blood from their victims, they meant much more than just physical blood. As they understood the word, blood-sucking vampires were also feeding upon a subtle substance intricately wound up with the vital, spiritual force of life itself.

Even in the folklore, it is not just about blood. There is a crucial exchange between vampire and victim, an intimate sharing of vitality and life-force that goes far beyond the physical realm. It is this subtle, elusive exchange that defines the vampire more than any other single thing. The blood is the life, but it is the life which sustains us. The passion for night-tide, the sun-sensitive eyes, the fangs -- these things are just trappings when compared to that one thing. What makes a vampire? A vampire must feed. Be it blood, sex, life force, *chi*, or *prana* -- that one distinction connects all the many breeds one may encounter today.

Blutsauger: A variety of vampire local to East Prussia who was reputed to prize the blood of young women. The word, in German, means literally, "blood-drinker."

Brahmaparush: An Indian species of vampire with particularly gruesome habits. The *brahmaparush* is not satisfied with simply killing its prey. It tears off the skull, makes a cup of it, and from this grisly chalice drinks the victim's blood. The *brahmaparush* is also known to dance upon the corpse of its victim, wearing their intestines like a kind of turban, wrapped around its head. In these habits, the *brahmaparush* is very similar to the *dakinis* described in the *Tibetan Book of the Dead.* These fierce and beautiful women, sometimes depicted with an animal head, are often blood-drinkers, and many hold in their hand a chalice made from a skull from which they drink the precious blood.

Bruxsa: A Portuguese spirit, whose name is clearly related to the Spanish word, *bruja*, for witch. The *bruxsa* is indeed a witch, and like many of the vampiric witches from other cultures, she has the ability to shapeshift. At night, she becomes a large bird, and it is in this form that she goes about causing trouble and drinking blood. The *bruxsa* not only feeds upon children – she is very cannibalistic in nature, preferring the blood of her own offspring above all others.

Cain: Biblical figure, first-born son of Adam and Eve. In Genesis, Cain is attributed with the first murder. He and his younger brother Abel were to offer gifts for sacrifice to the Lord God. Abel, as he was a shepherd, offered the blood of a fine young lamb. Cain, a farmer, offered the first and best fruits of his harvest. The Lord God, who had cursed the land and all that sprang forth from it, preferred the offering of blood. Cain, jealous of the preferential treatment given to his brother, sought Abel out in the fields and slew him. Cain was then cursed by God and sent out into the world to wander. He was given a Mark by which all would recognize him and know that the Lord God prevented him from harm. It is suggested that Cain was made immortal, for God makes it clear that no man can kill him, and from this story, a slew of folktales arose. In the Middle Ages, Cain was equated with the Wandering Jew, a mysterious figure, also believed to be immortal, attributed with magickal powers and questionable motives. In the nineteenth century, Lord Byron took up the case of Cain, making him into one of his strangely gifted and compelling outcast heroes and putting him on a level with Lucifer and Manfred. It is unclear when Cain became a part of vampire myth, but by 1982, the novel *Fevre Dream* by George R. Martin depicts Cain as the forefather of a race of evil vampires. White Wolf, in its role-playing game *Vampire: the Masquerade*, took up the figure of Cain and made him the first vampire from which all the rest are descended, a move which has solidified Cain as a key figure in vampire mythology ever since.

Chiang-shi: The Chinese believe that there are two distinct parts of the soul in any human body. The *hun*, which is the higher soul, is the part which moves on to a new incarnation upon death. The *p'o*, or lower soul, is attached to the body and can be kept from moving onward if there are seriously unresolved issues from the previous life. The *p'o* is most likely to become earth-bound if a body was improperly buried, or if the person it belonged to was a very evil person in life. In rare occasions, the *p'o* will stay behind and reanimate the body, and when this happens, the *chiang-shi* is the result. The *chiang-shi* is generally tall and has white or greenish hair all over its body. In addition to this, it has wicked claws, glowing eyes, and fangs. Like some European vampires, the *chiang-shi* can be stopped by sprinkling grains of rice, bits of iron, or many tiny red beans on top of its grave.

Chupacabra: A relatively recent newcomer to the canon of vampiric entities, this South American boogeyman is believed to suck the blood from goats and other livestock. Its name, appropriately enough, means, "goat-sucker." From the nineties onward, there have been sightings of this ghastly creature, which looks in alleged photos like a malformed, hairless dog. As is perhaps fitting for a folkloric creature that had its birth in the twentieth century, most people do not ascribe the *chupacabra* with a strictly supernatural character, believing it to be some kind of space alien instead.

Civatateo: An Aztec noblewoman, dying in childbirth, was in danger of becoming a *civatateo*. With hideous white faces, white chalk covering their arms and hands, and symbols of death painted upon their clothes, the *civatateo* were believed to roam about at night, gathering particularly at crossroads. Like many spirits which issued from women doomed in childbirth, the *civatateo* returned to feed upon the children of others. They were considered very dangerous, but they were also respected as the servants of a pair of moon deities, Tezcatlipoca and Tlazolteotl. For this reason, shrines were left to them, and those who wanted to sate the spirits' hunger for children's blood and flesh would leave offerings of food in the shrine in the hopes of appeasing them.

Crowley, Aleister: It is said in one of his follower's memoirs that Crowley had his eyeteeth filed to resemble fangs. He would greet ladies not by kissing them on their hands, as was the custom in his day, but by taking their wrists and biting into them. He referred to this as "the serpent's kiss." Never the sort to be timid, Crowley practiced blood magick and sex magick, sometimes intermingling the two in an unprecedented sado-sexual style that both horrified and titillated the media of the day. Leila Waddell, Crowley's first partner for work in sex magick, was ritually scarred by Crowley with his mark, the so-called "Mark of the Beast," in the area just over her heart. Crowley had many lovers, and judging from what many of them have said of him in personal letters and memoirs, Crowley's fascination for blood and blood magick would make him quite at home with today's modern blood fetishists. The activities of Crowley and his lovers had the lot of them expelled from Italy shortly after Crowley had founded the Abbey of Thelema in Cefalu, Sicily. For similar reasons, Crowley and his newest mistress, Maria Theresa de Miramar, were expelled from France in 1929.

Dakini: A terrible and beautiful demi-goddess from the Tibetan tradition. The *dakinis* appear to a person during the process of dying, and they are part of the long visionary journey that ensues after physical death and before the deceased chooses to reincarnate. The *dakinis* are ambivalent beings for they appear in frightening and terrible forms to the deceased, but only in order to get the dead person to address issues about his past life and resolve his attachments so he can move on to a higher existence. Many of the *dakinis* are vampiric in nature, being described as naked women, sometimes with the heads of animals, who drink blood from chalices made of human skulls. The *dakinis* appear with the Peaceful and Wrathful Deities, beings who, like the *dakinis*, exhibit ghastly vampiric natures in an attempt to convince the deceased of the impermanency of the flesh.

Dearg-dul: A vampiric spirit from Irish faerie lore, the *dearg-dul* is a beautiful woman who rises from her grave, seeking lovers to clasp in her embrace. Anyone foolish enough to go to her will pay for his folly with his life. The only way to stop this deadly beauty once she appears is to locate the grave by which she enters this world and cover it up with a cairn of heavy stones. According to Jackson, her name means, "red blood-sucker."

Demons: There are many demonic beings throughout world myth and folklore which are attributed with vampiric abilities. In general the thing which distinguishes a demon from a vampire is its wholly inhuman nature. A demon is not and never was human; it is of a separate order of beings from humanity. Vampires have their beginnings in humanity, even though some cultures believe that for a corpse to rise again it must be possessed by a demonic spirit. Still, the body which the spirit inhabits is human, and the guise it wears when it appears to its victims is that of the dead man or woman.

Dhampir: A child, always male, who is the product of a vampire and a mortal. Usually a dhampir has a vampiric father and a mortal mother. Most dhampirs are conceived when a husband dies, but as a vampire he returns to visit his wife at night. Dhampirs are mortal, but they possess the ability to sense vampires, and thus they are believed to make excellent vampire hunters. In Europe, where the vampire folklore flourished, dhampirs were in high demand, and many could make their living traveling from town to town, putting their vampiric heritage to work by determining which graves in the local cemeteries were inhabited by vampires. The vampires within were then dug up, and the dhampir helped the townspeople destroy them.

Draugr: A figure from old Norse legends, the *draugr* is known as a "deathwalker." This inimical being is a risen corpse who has been called up, zombie-like, by some magician who then dispatches it on errands of death.

Egyptian Vampires: The ancient Egyptians had a very complex and detailed vision of the afterlife. Their concept of the soul was equally complex, assigning each person several different souls. The *Ba,* depicted as a bird with a human head, represented the life force, and it was this bird that flew forth from the body at the time of death. The *Akh,* represented by the eternally reborn Benu bird (phoenix), is the immortal or undying soul. And finally, the *Ka,* is the part of the soul that is tied to the body and remains in the tomb after burial. Like the Chinese *p'o*, the Egyptian Ka could sometimes become tied to the body and bring it to a second life. It is for the *Ka* that the family and priests offer gifts and foodstuffs, for if it is not appeased by these things, it can go forth from the tomb and seek its sustenance from the living.

In addition to earth-bound Ka-spirits, the Egyptians also believed in a number of demonic entities which they called the *Amam*, or Devourers. These were disincarnate entities which lay in wait for souls traveling through the netherworld. Each *Amam* had a favorite part of the body which it liked to devour, such as *Amam-arit,* who ate only eyeballs, and *Amam-senf* who drank human blood. There are many spells and incantations listed in the *Egyptian Book of the Dead* intended to protect a person's soul from attack by these inimical creatures.

Ekimmu: In ancient Sumeria and Babylon, the spirits of the dead were believed to take the form of people with bird's wings. When spirits were not given sufficient offerings of water at family shrines or if they were bound by a violent death or some misdeed, they became restless. Restless spirits could harm the living, feeding upon their life. In the *Epic of Gilgamesh*, Enkidu describes an encounter with one such horrific entity: "I stood before an awful being, the somber-faced man-bird. His was a vampire face, his foot was a lion's foot, his hand was an eagle's talon. He fell on me, and his claws were in my hair. He held me fast, and I smothered."

Empusa: A vampiric spirit from Greece, the *empusa* has no set form of its own but can take on any shape it likes in order to lure people to it. Like many vampiric entities, the *empusa* seems to like taking on the shape of an attractive young woman, as this tends to net the most prey. Once someone has approached it, the *empusa* enters their body, feeding upon their flesh and blood until they sicken and die. Classical writers Philostratus and Aristophanes both record details about *empusas.*

Ereticy: In Russia, the *ereticy* are old women who sold their soul to the Devil or people who were excommunicated for heresy in the Church. Such heretical beings arose as vampires after their death, and were thought to sleep in the coffins of the impious. The *ereticy* were attributed with the evil

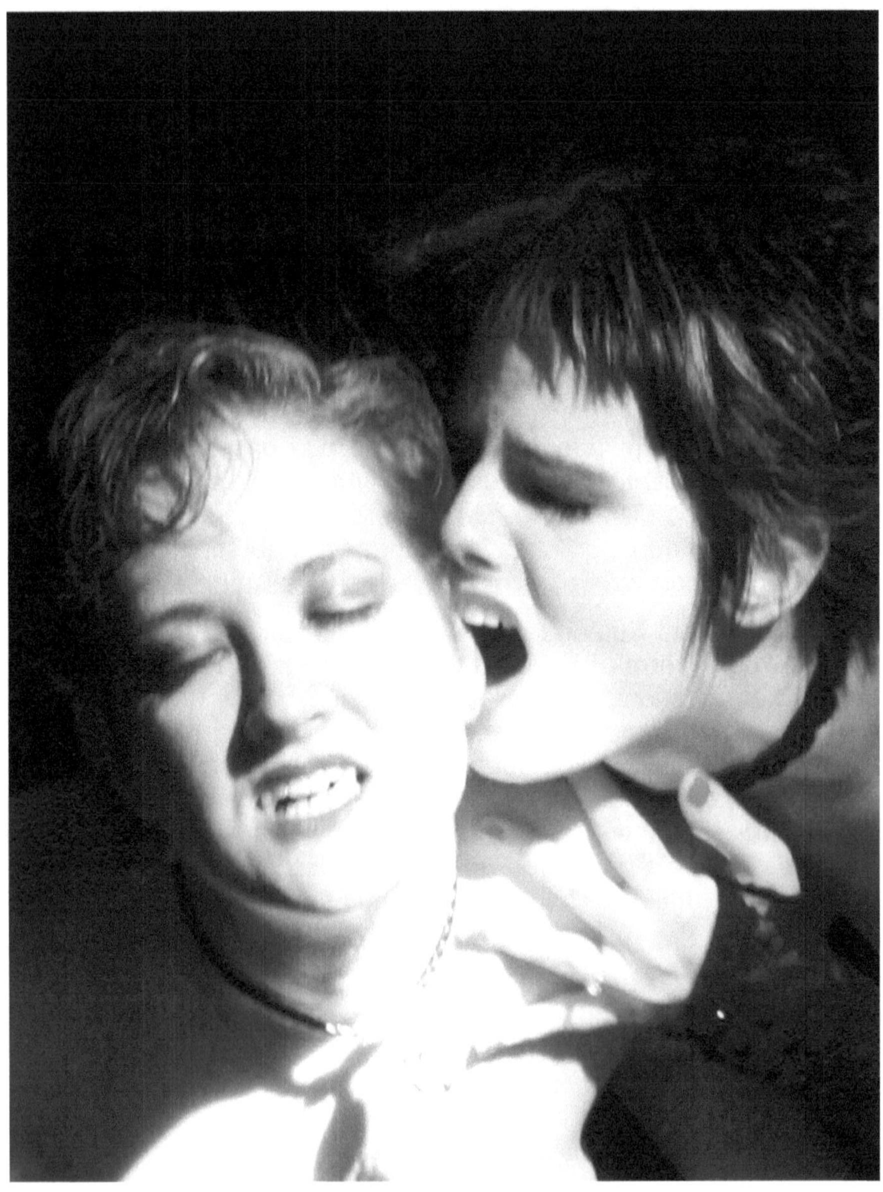

eye and coming into contact with one generally guaranteed that you were doomed to waste away and die.

Estrie: A vampiric female entity from Hebrew myth. The *estrie* was an evil spirit which took up a body so that it could better prey upon humanity. *Estrie* drink blood and prefer that of children, although they will attack men and women as well. When such a vampire dies, the grave is watched for a year thereafter, just in case the creature continues its predations. Usually this watchful period can be circumvented by placing soil in the mouth of the corpse, an activity which renders the spirit powerless.

Female Vampires: While male vampires in folklore are often horrific, female vampires are frequently described as beautiful and seductive. In folklore the world over, female vampires share many things in common. Often they are the restless spirits of mothers whose children have died or who have died trying to bring a life into this world. Because they died through childbearing, female vampires are often condemned to feed upon children. In death, these mournful mothers become ravishing, and their bitter anger is taken out not only upon the children they were denied, but upon the men who burdened them with those children in the first place. Many female vampires seduce young men, sometimes going as far as marrying them, only to feed upon them later. Interestingly, these vampiric spirits are also often associated with water and the color green. The Malaysian *langsuir* and the Scottish *baobhan-sith* both appear wearing robes of green.

Fifollet: The Cajun population of Louisiana tell of a dancing light in the bayou that leads wanderers astray. When they sink in the muck, this ethereal being descends and feeds upon them. Derived from the French *feu-follet,* or "spritely fire," this vampiric will o' the wisp is reputed to especially enjoy the blood of children.

Garlic: Long thought to be the bane of vampires, garlic was used all across Europe to ward away evil spirits of all descriptions. Cloves of garlic were hung about doors to keep evil spirits out, and frequently garlic was stuffed into the mouth of a corpse suspected of being a vampire. Interestingly enough, garlic is used today in homeopathic medicine as a blood-cleanser, a fact which in some peoples' minds ties it even more thoroughly to vampires and vampirism. In addition to garlic, other apotropaics believed to ward off vampires and evil spirits included wold roses, hawthorne, ash, rowan, juniper, and holly. Wolfsbane, known also as aconite and Monk's Hood, was yet another plant thought to ward off vampires. This was a potent talisman against werewolves as well.

Gayal: Another vampiric spirit from India, the *gayal* is the spirit of a man who has died unmarried or without a male heir to perform his funeral rites. Thus deprived of rest, the *gayal* takes out his ire on the sons of others, much as vampiric female spirits who died in childbirth subsequently seek out the infants of others to satisfy their hunger. Living mothers place a coin around the neck of their own sons to protect them from this spirit and leave out offerings of milk and Ganges water in the hopes of appeasing him.

Gelal: In ancient Sumeria, one of a number of vampiric entities who haunt the wastelands and sap the vitality from the living. Gelal is mentioned in reference to the *lilitu*, the company of evil spirits to which Lilith belonged.

Ghost: In general, a ghost is a human spirit which, for one reason or another, has become restless after death. Ghosts are differentiated from vampires mainly by the fact that they do not need to drink blood or steal life force and they tend to never have a corporeal form.

Hannya: A feared and oft-depicted Japanese demon, the *hannya* was believed to be a very beautiful woman who had, for one reason or another, gone insane. Her madness allowed a demon to possess her, and this rendered her hideously ugly and fearsome. *Hannya*, like many female vampires, was supposed to drink the blood of children, especially relishing that of infants. In the No drama of Japan, however, the *hannya* is more often depicted as a lamia-like seducer of young men.

Incubus: In the Classical world, there was a widespread divinatory practice called *incubation*. In this process, the person seeking answers would go to a special oracle or a tomb, sacrifice a sheep, skin it, then go to sleep on the fleece. It was believed that the gods or the spirits of the dead would then visit the querent in his sleep and grant him a dream-vision of what he was seeking. The spirit that would appear to an individual practicing incubation was known as an incubus.

In the Medieval world, all the daemons and spirits that the Greeks and Romans sought for guidance were transformed into demons. Accordingly, in the folklore of Medieval Europe, the Incubus became a male demon who seduced young women in order to have sex with them. Retaining some connection with the notion of incubation, the Incubus would generally begin by appearing in the victim's dreams. Here, he would inspire erotic and lustful thoughts.

The creature was not thought to be limited purely to dreams, however. An incubus was believed to have sufficient power to visit its victim in a physical form and therefore complete the acts which it only hinted at in the dreams. Children could be born out of these unions, and they were invariably attractive, proud, tall, cunningly intelligent, and strong but with wicked appetites. The Succubus was the female counterpart to the Incubus.

Father Lodovico Sinistrari, a 17th century Italian monk, wrote an entire treatise on these beings, depicting them as a separate species from humanity whose body, rather than being made of gross physical matter, was made up of subtle energies. He attributed to both Incubi and Succubi elemental essences, so that some had a nature allied with fire while others might have a watery or even earthy nature. Father Sinistrari went on to postulate that Incubi and Succubi could in some instances reproduce with human beings, but that the children of Incubi and Succubi, although possessing a physical body, also retained some of the subtle nature of their non-human parent, and like that parent, fed upon the sexual or life energies of other humans they took as their lovers.

Jaracacas: A Brazilian spirit that appears in the form of a large snake. It delights in the taste of women's breast-milk, and will slither up their bellies and lay upon their chests to feed.

Katakhana: A vampire from Crete, related to the *vyrkolakas.* Like the *vyrkolakas*, the *katakhana* was believed to have been an evil person in life whose body, as a result of this evil, was inhabited by a demonic spirit after its death.

Kephn: A Burmese vampire which, like the *aswang*, is a living person by day. The *kephn* is a sorcerer or wizard who is able to cahnge shape. When the *kephn* goes out to feed, it appears as a disembodied head with a stomach trailing from it. The *kephn* does not drink the blood of its victims. Getting straight to the point, this ghastly being utterly devours the person's soul.

Kresnik: One of a pair of Slovenian beings believed to be locked in an epic struggle of good versus evil. The *kresnik* is described by Senn as a "sunheor" who guards the house or village against werewolves. Alternately, the *kresnik* is a vampire who does about the same, rising from its grave at night to chase evil spirits away. Under certain circumstances, however, the *kresnik* itself could be evil. These beings are described as sometimes appearing in the form of a lynx, which creates a curious animal opposition between them and the wolf-like *kudlaks.*

Kudlak: Variant spelling of the *vlkodlak,* a word originally used for werewloves but later used to mean "vampire." Bunson describes this creature as an evil being who worked in opposition to the good *kresnik.* By this reckoning of things, the *kudlak* was a living vampire and a shapeshifter who worked for the powers of evil to cause mischief throughout the village. The *kresnik* was more or less the same kind of being, except the *kresnik's* powers were used for the protection of the village. Inevitably, these two beings clashed, often in epic struggles that involved successive transformations through their various animal forms.

K'uei: In Chinese lore, the *k'uei* is a malevolent spirit that can adversely affect the energy of a place. Like most demons and evil spirits in Chinese lore, *k'uei* are believed to only travel in straight lines. The distinctive shape of a traditional Chinese roof was constructed to help divert evil spirits and related energies away from the temple, palace, or home. Another diversionary tactic involved placing a screen across a door that the *k'uei* could not get around. Jackson suggests that the low walls built around temple complexes in South Asia were also used to keep such evil influences out.

Kukudhi: An Albanian term for the last and most powerful stage of the vampire. Apparently, the Albanians believed that once a person had become a vampire, there were various stages of development in which they realized their powers. The *kukundhi* then was the eldest and most mature form of the vampire. Once a vampire had reached this state, it was no longer consigned to return to its grave but could live at home just like an ordinary person. It could also travel to foreign lands if it so desired, generally in the disguise of a merchant.

Lamia: A vampiric being from Greek myth. Lamia was once queen of Libya. She was both very beautiful and very proud. Zeus came to her as a lover, and she bore children from their union. However, the always jealous goddess Hera, wife of Zeus, found out about their affair and struck down the children of Lamia. Lamia swore thereafter to destroy the children of others in revenge. Other Greek sources, however, depict the lamia as a young woman who seduces young men in order to destroy them. One such, whose nature was revealed on the very night of the wedding feast, provided inspiration for Keats' famous poem "Lamia." Most *lamia* are depicted as having deformed lower limbs, and in modern depictions this has developed into portraying them as having a serpent-like lower body, much like a *naga*.

Lampir: A Bosnian vampire who is especially active during epidemics of typhus. *Lampirs* are able to return at night to their living spouses in order to drink their blood and have sex with them. Children born of these unions are called *lampijerovics.* Bearing much in common with *dhampirs, lampijerovics* possess a unique ability for sensing the undead and are therefore often used to hunt them down and destroy them. Jackson tells of a village in the district of Novopazarski Sandzak that is almost completely populated by *lampijerovics*, all of whom claim to be descended from the same vampire.

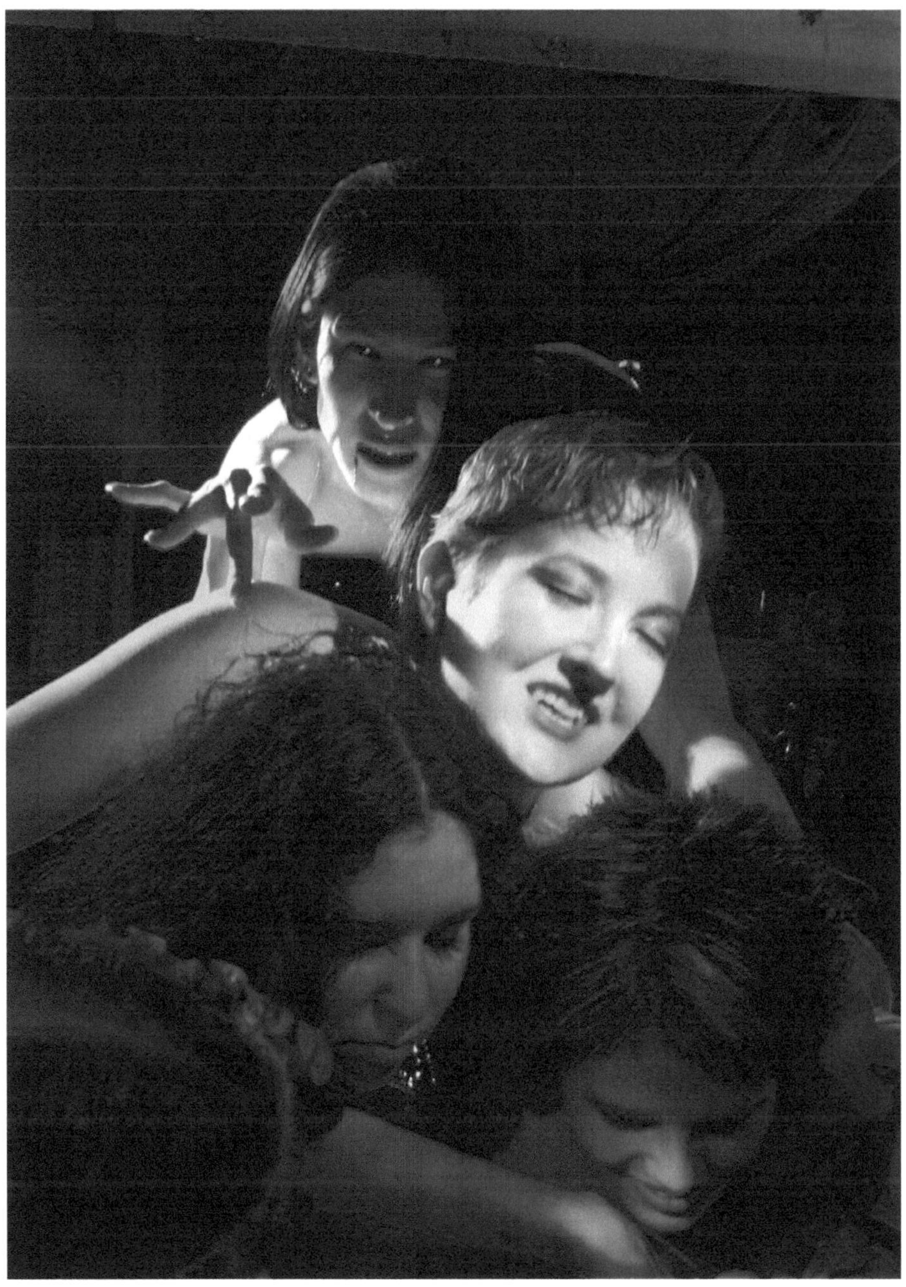

Langsuir: A Malaysian demon and the female counterpart of the *bajang.* A *langsuir* is created when a woman dies in childbirth or through other complications of pregnancy. After forty days, her corpse flies out of its grave unless needles have been driven through her arms to prevent this. At this point, she becomes wild, her hair grows long and unkempt, and her fingernails grow like talons. She also has a curious hole in the back of her neck, although this is covered by her wild hair.

Like the *Baobhan-sith* and the *Leanan-sidhe*, she is incredibly beautiful and she is almost always clad in robes of green. She is known for the terrible wailing sound she makes, called the *ngilai* in Malaysia. She and her sisters often haunt rivers, for *langsuir* crave fish in addition to sucking the blood of children. To overcome this vampire, you must cut off her hair and fingernails and stuff them into the hole in the back of her neck. After this, she will become quite docile, and can even be married like an ordinary woman.

Leanan-Sidhe: Another vampiric faerie from the British Isles. Like her Scottish counterpart, the *baobhan-sith,* the *leanan-sidhe* appears as a beautiful young woman and she is quite fond of seducing young men. Her name means “the fairy girl-friend,” and on the Isle of Man, she is also considered to be a kind of muse. She feeds upon promising young poets and artists, seducing them and drinking their blood. Over the course of many months, she appears to them again and again, inspiring their art but also sapping their health and vitality. The young men who fall under her spell burn brilliantly like a star, and then wink out, all their light and vitality spent in her deadly arms.

Lilith: Perhaps the earliest being attributed with powers we would associate with a vampire was the demonic entity known as Lilith. Lilith was originally a Sumerian creature who is first referenced as a spirit haunting a tree. As part of the *lilin* or *lilitu,* she was a taloned and winged demon associated with wild beasts and waste places. She and her kind were believed to harm women during pregnancy, interfere with labor, and kill infants in their cribs. The Babylonians inherited Lilith from their cultural predecessors, the Sumerians, and, during the Babylonian captivity, Lilith was picked up by the Hebrews.

In the mythology of the Israelites, Lilith underwent some major changes. She was adopted into Rabbinical lore where she became the first wife of Adam. As the tradition goes, originally, the Lord God made his Adam, then split him into two beings: Adam and Lilith. Lilith was not so much made out of a part of Adam as she was just a female counterpart to the first man. In this respect, she was his equal in all things. Her major “flaw”, and the "sin" that got her expelled from Eden, was the fact that she was headstrong and demanded equality. She did not want to be treated as Adam's inferior and she refused to take orders from him. This streak of feminism did not much please Adam or his male God, and so Lilith found herself sent packing into the wilderness. Once she was gone, the Lord God created a more docile partner for Adam out of his rib.

Opinions differ on what happened to Lilith after she was expelled from Eden. Most stories agree that she did not die but flourished in the wastelands. It is said that she became the first demon, spawning all the rest from her willful essence (of course, if Lilith is a demon and she's just a female counterpart of Adam, that makes humanity very confused about its actual nature). Other traditions maintain that she became the wife of Lucifer. Still other stories relate how she took up residence in the land of Nod, and there eventually found and seduced Cain, the prodigal son of Adam. Most traditions agree that Lilith eventually developed a thirst for blood. In the Rabbinical lore, she retains some of the characteristics she had in her old Sumerian incarnation. She is associated strongly with wild beasts, and is described as having long, wild, unkempt hair. She is still often depicted as winged and taloned, rather like a harpy or a strige. She is still believed to feed upon infants, snatching them away from their mothers in the night. She is also believed to seduce men, luring them with her wiles then devouring them when they are at their most vulnerable.

Loogaroo: A West Indies vampire whose name is very probably derived from the French *loup garou*, or werewolf. Like the *loup garou*, the *loogaroo* is a shapeshifter. By day, she is a woman, usually old. At night, she takes off her skin so that she is nothing more than a glowing light. In this will o' the wisp-like form, she will go about her village, seeking a victim from whom she will suck blood. If she is harmed in her shifted form, the wound will show up on her regular body once she changes back. This is the best method of identifying her.

Mandurugo: Another vampire which originates in the Philippines. The *mandurugo*, whose name means "bloodsucker", is a beautiful woman by day but can effect a ghastly transformation at night, flying through the air in search of blood. Most *mandurugo* seem to have a very practical streak to them, as many will seduce a man and marry him, thereby securing for themselves a constant supply of blood. Even a married *madurugo* will get bored once in a while and leave her husband's side to go off flying about and drinking more varied fare. According to Matthew Bunson, a *mandurugo* was seen in the Philippines as recently as the 1992 presidential election.

Mara: A European spirit who visits victims at night and steals their breath. The victim of a mara attack feels paralyzed and cannot move or even scream, but feels a terrible foreboding during the whole experience. Mara attacks, sometimes known as "hag attacks" have been explained in modern days as a phenomenon associated with dreams and sleep. While you are sleeping, your body is paralyzed so that you cannot act out your dreams. Sometimes this paralyzation takes hold prior to REM sleep while the individual is still more or less conscious. An oppressive sensation and something like a panic attack usually accompany this, giving rise to the sensation of being attacked. Some sufferers of these "hag attacks" report that they felt they were being pressed into the bed by a great weight. In metaphysical communities, hag attacks are viewed as sometimes resulting from psychic attack, particularly of the sort that comes from being visited by an astral vampire in ones sleep.

Moroi: Romanian term used to distinguish a living vampire from the undead variety. A *moroi* is a living person with many of the abilities often attributed to undead vampires. They rarely directly drink human blood but are capable of sapping the vitality of others from a distance. One tale of a *moroi* explains how, with a look at a man who had offended him, the *moroi* caused blood to begin seeping from his anus. Unlike many sorcerers or witches, *moroi* do not choose to become what they are. It is believed that they are cursed (or blessed) with their powers from birth. Invariably, when a living vampire passes away, he is believed to return as an undead vampire, or *strigoi,* after death.

Mullo: A Gypsy vampire, the *mullo* is someone who died by violence or who was restless because their burial rites were not properly performed. *Mullo*, when they rise, generally look precisely the same way as they did in life, although sometimes they can be identified for what they are because their hair has grown so long it nearly brushes the ground. *Mullo* wake with an astonishing sexual appetite, and they will seek out their former lovers and exhaust them with sexual demands. Those that the *mullo* visits in this way will often sicken and die themselves, as the strain of meeting the *mullo's* sexual desires is simply too much for a mortal to handle. Children can be born from the union of a *mullo* and its partner, and these are almost always *dhampirs*. The *mullo* is also driven by a need to avenge itself on those it disliked in life, and sustains itself by strangling humans or livestock and drinking their blood. A *mullo* is very hard to destroy, but they have a limited lifespan after they have risen from the grave, and after a period of a few years, they will return to the place where they rose, sink into the ground, and stir no more.

Muroni: A Wallachian vampire, the *muroni* is a deft shapeshifter. Able to take on the shape of a cat, dog, spider, or even a flea, the *muroni* is thus able to disguise its attacks. The victim of the *muroni*, however, is left completely drained of blood, a circumstance which would be curious (to say the least) if brought about by any ordinary spider or flea. Victims of the *muroni* are condemned in their own turn to become vampires, the only "cure" being a stake through the heart or a long nail through the center of the forehead. The name of this vampire is curiously close to *Moroni,* the name of an angel in Mormon sacred literature.

Nachzehrer: Literally a "gnawing corpse", the *nachzehrer* is a Germanic kind of vampire. The *nachzehrer*, upon waking in its grave, begins to gnaw on things. First it gnaws upon its funeral shroud, then its own lips and sometimes its own fingers. Supposedly, if you pass by the grave of a particularly active *nachzehrer*, you will hear the incessant grinding sound of its teeth as it chews away on everything. As the *nachzehrer* chews, family members who are still living sicken and die. It is unclear whether the *nachzehrer* was believed to actually leave its grave and prey upon the living or if the very act of its chewing in the grave had a sympathetic affect of devouring those it once loved. In either case, in order for the sickness and death brought about by this creature to end, it had to be dug up and thoroughly destroyed.

Nelapsi: A Czechoslovakian vampire who is fearsome indeed. The *nelapsi* is believed to have two hearts, and therefore two souls. At death, one soul flies forth while the other remains to animate the body. The *nelapsi* does quite a bit more than simply steal forth from its grave and drink peoples' blood. This particular kind of vampire can slay whole villages, men, women, children, and livestock, in order to slake its thirst. It is also capable of killing a man with a single glance. Anyone who falls within the creature's line of sight when he invokes this powerful version of the Evil Eye are in danger of dropping over dead.

Nephilim: The Nephilim are half-breed beings, part angelic and part human, who are referred to in the *Book of Enoch I.* According to the 17th century writer Lodovico Sinistrari, Nephilim and any other children that share part of an otherworldly parentage are typically tall, powerful, and long-lived. In addition to this, they tend to be very charismatic, but with a cruel streak that predisposes them to evil. Another term given to the Nephilim in the Biblical texts translates to "men of renown," as they were believed to naturally be leaders among men.

The *Book of Enoch* tells us that the Nephilim and their angelic fathers were responsible for teaching mankind all of the arts and sciences that had previously been reserved for the gods alone: metallurgy, herbalism, warfare, divination, and various forms of magick. According to the *Book of Enoch*, the Nephilim's reign upon the Earth was the prime reason for the Flood. It is said that they drank one another's blood as well as the blood of the ordinary humans over whom they ruled. Eventually, their appetites became so great that they were devouring everything, including one another. The Lord God was compelled by the other angels to wipe the Nephilim's taint from the earth. Many modern-day vampires identify themselves with the Nephilim, at least in a metaphorical sense. They see themselves as coming from humanity yet touched by something which has lifted them above their simple human beginnings.

Neuntoter: A Saxon vampire whose name means "nine-killer". The name is thought to have come from the fact that it takes this creature nine days to mature in the grave until it is ready to go forth and wreak harm. The *neuntoter* is renown for its ability to bring plagues and it is believed that the best way of destroying it is to place a lemon in its mouth.

Nosferatu: A lustful species of Romanian vampire, the *nosferatu* is thought to be the illegitimate child of parents who were themselves illegitimate. Like the *mullo*, once the *nosferatu* rises from its grave, it does not content itself only with drinking blood. The creature have a rapacious love for orgies with the living, and the male *nosferatu* are able to get children upon their female victims. Children sired in this way will invariably be living vampires (*moroi)* or witches in their lives and are doomed to rise as vampires upon their own deaths. *Nosferatu* are very jealous of those who enjoy the bliss of wedlock as well, often seeking out newly married couples and striking the man with impotency and making the wife barren.

Obayifo: A kind of living vampire who is also a witch. In African lore, the *obayifo* sucks the blood of children from a distance, causing them to weaken and die. The *obayifo* is also able to suck the vitality from the land, bringing blights upon the crops. Their favorite crop is cacao.

Oboroten: A type of Russian vampire cited by Senn and said to compare to the *volkodlak*.

Omuli: (plural, avali): Among the Nande of Zaire, there is a belief in the *omuli*, literally, "one who eats." The *omuli* is a girl or woman, typically quite beautiful, who goes out at night devours peoples' souls. The *omuli* often chooses her victim out of jealousy or revenge. Then she sends her own spirit out and visits her victim while he or she sleeps. Through her *omuli* powers, she draws her victim's life principle out of his or her body, often taking this back to her *omuli* sisters in the woods so they can share a communal meal. The victim may not die immediately, but will gradually waste away of "consumption."

According to the Nande, one becomes an *omuli* by choice, but can eventually forswear the practice. Initiation as an *omuli* usually requires that the young woman bring one soul as a sacrifice for the others to eat. Typically, this is a member of her own family.

Penanggalan: A Malaysian vampire very similar to the *aswang* mentioned above. The *penanggalan* is a female entity, described as a disembodied head and neck with the viscera trailing along behind it.

The origins and exact nature of the *penanggalan* are not entirely clear. Some stories say that she was a woman who died in childbirth. Others attest that she was a woman who was performing some sort of religious penance and when the sanctity of her duty was interrupted by a man, she tore her head off and yanked her intestines out and flew away, wailing. These cases would suggest that the *penanggalan* is only one woman in particular, but other stories suggest that, like the *aswang*, the *penanggalan* is more of a separate species. She can appear to be an ordinary villager by day, only making her hideous transformation at night. It is said that she uses copious amounts of vinegar the next morning in order to shrink her bloated intestines up so that she can fit them back into her body when she reattaches her head. The *penanggalan* is believed to suck the blood of infants as well as attacking women in childbirth. Thorns and brambles are put on the roofs of houses where women are giving birth so that if a *penanggalan* comes, she will get her intestines caught on these and thus be unable to do any harm.

Pijawica: The Croatian word for the vampire, *pijawica* comes from the root *pit* meaning "to drink" and is also used to describe a hard-drinker. The Serbians and Slovaks also refer to a hard-drinker as a vampire or someone who has "the thirst of a vampire." Contrary to modern depictions of pallid nightwalkers, the folkloric vampire is often thought of as having a ruddy complexion. This belief was often reinforced when suspected vampires were dug up from their graves and their faces were seen to be ruddy because of a certain stage in the process of decay. An individual whose face bears the tell-tale burst blood vessels of a very hard drinker is often described as being "red as a vampire."

Polong: A Malaysian bottle imp, much like a *bajang*. However, where the main ingredient for creating a *bajang* involves a stillborn child, the *polong* requires the blood of a murderer for its creation. After the proper spells and incantations have been performed, the bottle in which the *polong* is to be

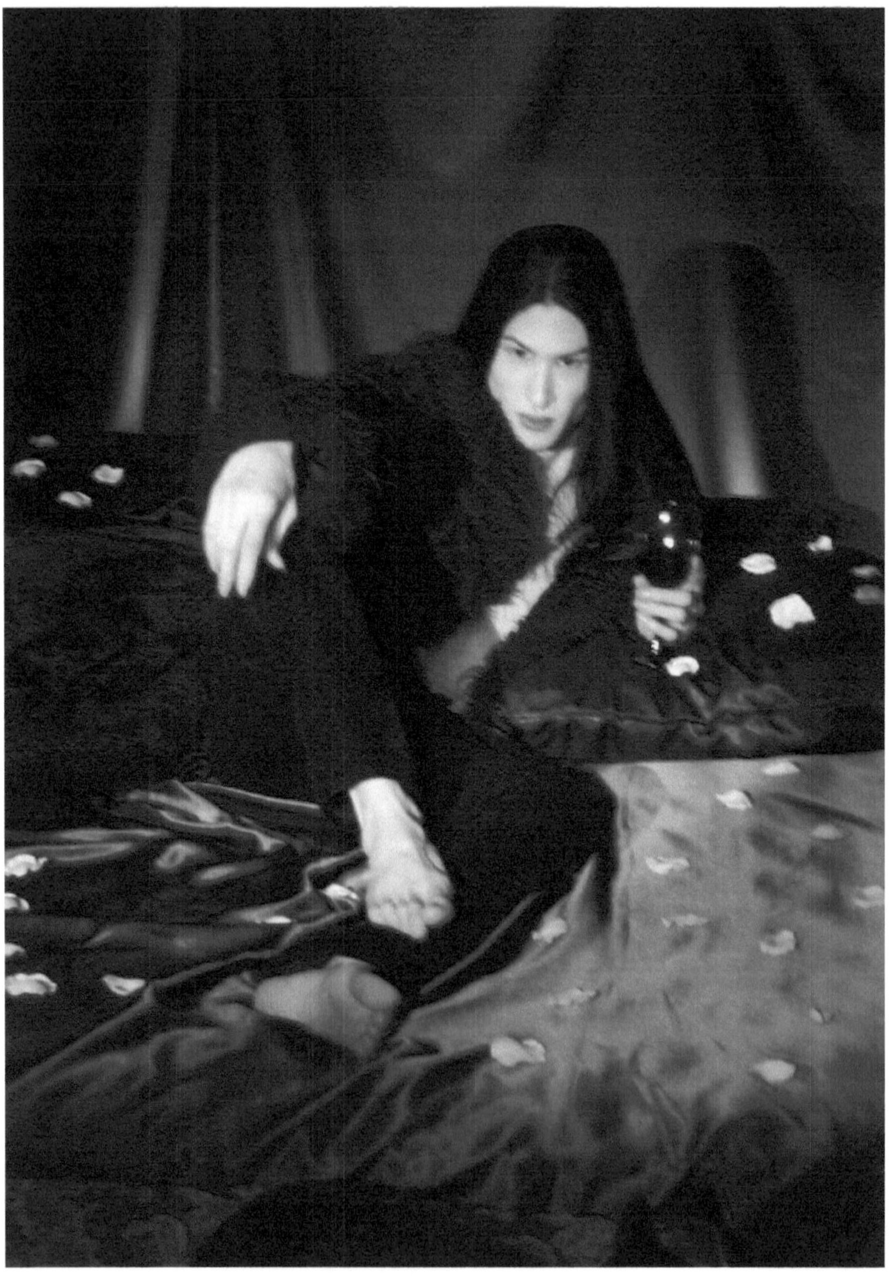

kept will issue forth with a sound like the chirping of birds. This indicates that the *polong* is present, and the magician who wishes to control it must then cut his finger and insert it into the bottle for the *polong* to suck. The magician must make this blood offering daily in order to solidify the bond between himself and the *polong*. Once matured, the *polong* can be sent forth to visit illness and death upon the magician's enemies. The *polong* has a familiar spirit, a cricket-like entity known as a *pelesit*. The *pelesit* goes forth to the victims and makes them ready for the *polong*, burrowing a small hole into their flesh through which the *polong* enters so it can suck their blood. If captured outside of its bottle, the *polong* has a striking appearance: that of a beautiful little woman, no larger than the last joint of the little finger.

Pontianak: When a mother dies in childbirth in Malaysia, she is believed to become a *langsuir*. The child which dies with its mother in such a birth becomes a *pontianak* Unless preventions are taken, the child will rise up and suck the life of the living. Stabbing a needle through the palm of each hand, filling the mouth with beads, and placing hen's eggs under each armpit will keep the unfortunate child quiet in the grave.

Pricolici: Romanian "inverted wolf." A man who is cursed to transform into a wolf at certain times. The time the man must transform into a wolf can be dictated by the seasons in addition to the more familiar phases of the moon. In most Eastern European countries, it is believed that an individual inflicted with lycanthropy can take control of his changes by donning a wolf pelt. He will turn into a wolf when he wears the pelt, and after spending some time as a wolf, he will revert back to his human state when he takes it off. Another common belief is that by drawing blood on an animal that is really a human transformed, the lycanthropic nature will be revealed and the person will change back to his or her natural state.

Psychic Vampires: Psychic vampires are people who, for one reason or another, feed off the energy of those around them. Many of these are unaware of their condition. However, there are some who have come to terms with what they are and can even control their vampirism. It is with these individuals where the distinction between the psychic and the astral vampire softens and blurs: many conscious psychic vampires can feed through a kind of astral projection, siphoning off energy from people in dreams or over long distances. Although they have a very mortal physical body, these exceptionally skilled psychic vampires have almost complete control over their astral bodies as well, and they can interact with the subtle reality as easily as many non-physical beings. Although they have abilities that some people might consider magickal (or complete nonsense, depending on what belief system you're coming from), but that does not necessarily make them supernatural. Psychic and astral vampires do require the life energy of others in order to sustain them, but ultimately, even their most ravenous appetites cannot kill someone. At worst, the victim of a prolonged astral / psychic vampire attack will get sick because their immune system can no longer take the strain of so much energy being sapped away.

Rakshasa: An Indian shapeshifter attributed with vampiric qualities. The *rakshasa* can transform themselves into vultures, dogs, eagles, and a variety of other things. Most often, however, they appear as humans with abnormally long tongues and intense, fiery eyes. Their throat is allegedly blue in color. In recent times, the *rakshasa* has somehow gotten connected with the tiger so that many who are familiar with the creature presume that its preferred form, when not human, is that of a man-tiger. Rakshasa have long, poisonous nails and are said to live in trees, causing nausea and vomiting in all who pass their territory at night. Other descriptions of these demonic beings portray them as blood stained with adamantine teeth and five legs.

Rusalye: A Slavic festival held on Pentecost to help procure the good will of those who had died a violent death. An integral part of the festival seems to be geared toward preventing the unquiet dead from rising again as vampires.

Rhode Island Vampires: A chilling case of vampirism struck the Tillinghast family of Rhode Island in the late 1790s. Sarah Tillinghast was a quiet solitary girl who had just turned nineteen. Suddenly she sickened, and after a protracted illness, passed away. After her passing, Sarah's siblings kept having dreams of her. She would visit them at night, complaining how cold she was. Each sibling who spoke of such dreams eventually sickened and died. Sarah's parents became convinced that the dead girl was somehow responsible. As was the custom, the girl's grave was dug up and her corpse summarily burned.

In 1883, the Brown family started on what was to be a long and tragic path of death. Mary Brown, wife of George, fell ill. Once a hearty woman, strengthened by farm work, she lost her life to consumption late in the year. A year later, Mary Olive, the eldest daughter died of the same wasting disease. Several years later, Edwin, Mary's only son, began to sicken. He left for Colorado Springs to convalesce, and his health improved. Shortly thereafter Mercy Brown, the youngest daughter grew ill. When she died, Edwin returned to Rhode Island, only to sicken shortly after arriving for the funeral. Vampirism was suspected, and on the morning of March 18, 1892, a good portion of the townspeople, accompanied by a doctor, opened the tomb of

Mercy Brown to determine whether she was the cause of her brother's renewed illness or not. Her heart and liver were found to be bloody, and these were removed and burned. Edwin passed away a few days later despite this precaution. Presumably, it came too late.

Samiu: Another term for the Devourers of Egyptian myth. The Devourers are disincarnate spirits, possibly human in origin, possibly demonic or divine, which haunt the netherworld and feast upon weak or guilty souls. Some of the Devourers are said to feast upon blood, some suck marrow from the bones, others eat excrement, and one eats only eyes.

Sburator: A draconian figure in Romanian folktales whose vampiric qualities inspired Raymond T. McNally to include him in the canon of Transylvanian vampires.

Stake, wooden: In modern film and fiction, we have developed the belief that a wooden stake driven directly through the heart of a vampire will paralyze it, and the creature will be unable to move until such time as the stake is removed. This has been adapted from the folklore in which a suspected vampire was almost literally nailed down in its grave. Sometimes actual nails or iron spikes were used, and sometimes it was a stake made of a wood, such a rowan or hawthorn. This was intended to keep the creature from rising, as it's hard to sit up in your coffin with a large chunk of something attaching you to the bottom of it. Sometimes, instead of being staked, the corpse was buried face-down in the coffin. If it woke to a new life in the grave, the upside-down corpse would start digging its way to the surface -- completely unaware of the trick that had been played, so that it only succeeded in digging itself further and further into the ground.

Striges: Yet another terrible female vampire who transforms herself at night and feeds upon the blood of children. *Striges* are believed to transform themselves into a crow or an owl. It is likely that the name comes from the Roman *strix* which was a screech owl. The Romans attributed to this bird a great capacity for malevolence and a fondness for drinking blood, especially that of infants. Ovid in particular describes the creatures as feeding upon babies.

Strigoi Vii, Strigoi Mort: "living witch," and "dead witch," respectively. In the Romanian material collected by folklorist Harry A. Senn, strigoi is used interchangeably to designate a witch or a vampire. The term "strigoi mort" represents vampires as they are more familiar to the pop cultural imagination, that is, as the walking dead. But quite often the qualifiers *"mort"* or *"vii"* are dropped entirely, and even living persons may be discussed as being vampires, as opposed to witches. The existence of these two terms, and the confusion surrounding them, is just one indication of the blurred lines that actually exist between werewolves, vampires, and witches in worldwide folkloric traditions. In the modern vampire subculture, *strigoi vii* has been adopted by the Elorathian tradition and some of what used to comprise the Sanguinarium to distinguish modern living vampires from those of literature or folklore.

Succubus: The female counterpart to the Medieval incubus. The succubus appears to her victims in fantasies and dreams, often also appearing in a physical form to exhaust them through wild orgies of sex. There is a distinct suggestion that the succubus has vampiric tendencies, as her victims always wake exhausted and drained from the night's activities.

Tebo (plural, *matebo*): an evil, vampiric spirit known to the Bakongo people of Western Zaire. The *tebo* may be the spirit of a sorcerer or other evil-doer who was denied entry to the afterlife by the clan ancestors. The *tebo* typically appears as an ugly dwarf with wrinkled, ash-colored skin. They may also appear as malformed and wrinkled children or as huge, fierce bats. Although they are restless spirits, they have a physical component, even though they are still able to appear and disappear at will due to various powers.

Wizards among the Bakongo people are believed to be the only ones who can capture the *tebo.* The trap is baited with human blood, and the wizard utters chants and conjurations to make it more alluring to the *tebo.* Come morning, a hungry and angry *tebo* will be visible in the trap.

If a *tebo* gets out of hand, it will attack people by sitting on their necks and drinking their blood. Only fire can destroy such a creature, and it must be destroyed utterly, so that no part of it is left, or else the remnant will merely grow into a new spirit.

Tricolici: Another supernatural creature from Romania that is sometimes associated with vampires and vampirism. Rather than being undead, however, the *tricolici* is a living man (or woman) who periodically turns into a pig or a dog. This were-pig or were-dog then attacks others, often attempting to suck their blood. Senn cites one report where a woman left her husband after it was revealed that he was a *tricolici.*

Ubour: A peculiar variety of Bulgarian vampire that drinks blood only when other food is unavailable to it. This unusual species of vampire has only one nostril and a barbed tongue. It is very easy to spot when it is out on its nightly forays, for it emits sparks in the darkness.

Upyr: A variety of Russian vampire with teeth as strong as iron which it uses to chew through obstacles. Most notably, these prodigious teeth are used by the creature to gain egress from its tomb during the winter, as its hands generally freeze in the cold earth and are entirely useless. The *upyr* feeds upon whole families, starting first with the children and then moving on to the parents. Like some vampires, the *upyr* is not limited to going out only at night, and is typically about doing its mischief from noon till midnight. The creature must be destroyed by a stake through the heart or by chopping off its head. Those who seek to destroy it, however, must see to it that they effect the staking or the decapitation with one blow only. If a second blow it struck, this will only bring the creature back to life and in a terrible fury.

Ustrel: A Bulgarian vampire which feeds exclusively on cattle. The *ustrel* is believed to be the spirit of a child who died unbaptized. After spending nine days in the ground, the *ustrel* claws its way out and makes it way to the nearest herd. Here it begins feeding upon the fattest and strongest animals first, working its way down to the weakest. Once the *ustrel* is strong enough, it no longer has to return to its grave, but prefers to sleep nestled up on one of the cows. The only way to rid the herd of this menace is to pass all the cattle in their turn through a need-fire.

Vampires, Feeding: While vampires are best known in pop culture for sucking blood, folklore does not restrict them to such sanguinary fare. In Romanian myth, it is believed that some vampires can suck the life from the grain. These vampires take their sustenance directly from the land, often leaving it barren and wasted as a consequence. Others are believed to suck milk from cows and sheep, sucking blood only when the milk has been exhausted. And the vampires do not need to go up to the cattle and actually, physically suck the milk from their dugs; the vampire responsible for feeding in this way may be miles distant from the herd being attacked. Sometimes cattle attacked in this manner will never produce milk again. Women are not exempt from this manner of predation and may find themselves preyed upon by a vampire who is after their breast milk. Breast milk plays a role in another aspect of vampire lore: in some societies, it is believed that if a child is weaned and then allowed to suckle again, he or she is foredoomed to rise as a vampire after death.

Vampires, Sexual: Some vampires are believed to return to their spouses and sexual partners after death, exhausting them with night-long marathons of sex. When dawn comes, the vampire lover flits away, only to return later in the night. The poor victims of these amorous assaults waste away and die from sheer exhaustion in a matter of weeks or even days. Such vampire lovers are believed to sometimes father children, who then are born as *dhampirs (page 116)*. If a widow whose husband has been dead more than nine months gives birth to a child, she can save face by saying that he visited her as a vampire.

Volkodlak: A Russian word for vampire, *volkodlak*, means "wolf-haired" or "wolf-skinned," and was originally used to describe a werewolf. The Bulgarian *vrkolak*, Serbian *vukolak*, Romanian *vircolac*, and Greek *vyrkolakas*, also originally referred to werewolves but now are used for vampires.

Vourdalak: Count Leo Tolstoy depicts this vampire, a variation on the Russian *volkodlak*, as a beautiful but evil woman. She appears in his short story, "The Family of the Vourdalak."

Walozi: Swahili word for "warlock". *Wazoli* are living men who devour peoples' souls. In Swahili, the word "roho" means both life and soul, and so the *walozi* are feeding on the life-essence of their victims, which in turn makes those victims sicken and die. *Walozi* are typically active at night and are able to leave their bodies so it seems as if they are merely asleep in their beds.

The *wazoli* did not choose to be what they are; it is believed that they were born with both the ability and the need to feast upon the soul-stuff of others. These life-stealing beings are known as *varoyi* in Zimbabwe, and *baloi* in Zambia, Botswana, and Lesotho.

Werewolf: In Romania especially, the distinction between vampires and werewolves is thin indeed. As demonstrated by *volkodlak* above, even the word for vampire may also be used to indicate a werewolf. The fact that many vampires are able to assume different shapes does not help clarify matters, either. It could be argued that werewolves are living while vampires are undead, yet in Romania alone there are many beliefs in living vampires – some of which are also believed to be able to change their shape. So how do we distinguish them? In general, werewolves are distinct from vampires in that they are shapeshifters exclusively. Also, while a werewolf is believed to be driven by a kind of frenzy to kill and devour people, they do this more to satisfy an urge or craving more than any legitimate need. The vampires of folklore, living or dead, rely upon blood or life-force in order to sustain themselves, and just as their victims weaken and die when repeatedly attacked, so too will the vampire weaken and expire if it is unable to gain its nightly sustenance.

Witch: Like the werewolf, the witches of folklore (and please let me distinguish this from modern witches or Wiccans!) are also often given vampiric or shapeshifting abilities, and it is hard to tell where the myths draw the line between one class of beings and the next. In general, folkloric witches are living humans believed to have supernatural abilities. Often, these abilities are gained from spirits which the witches control. Witches may enact spells which essentially mimic the symptoms of vampiric attack: their victims sicken, waste away, and eventually die. However, unlike the vampire, the witch's own vitality does not hinge upon the acting of stealing it from others. Witches typically attack others out of vengeance or jealousy, or because they have been paid by someone to do so.

Wieszczy: A vampire from Polish folklore who, like the *volkodlak* and many others, shares qualities in common with both vampires and werewolves.

Zmeu: McNally identifies this creature among his list of Transylvanian vampires. Senn insists that the *zmeu* is actually an ogress from Romanian fairytales. Bunson depicts the *zmeu* as some sort of sexual vampire. In Moldavia, the *zmeu* appears as a long, pale flame which follows a young girl or woman into her bedroom. Once in the room, the *zmeu* takes the form of a man and seduces the woman in question. In Transylvania, the *zmeu* is a young girl who appears to shepherds in the woods and offers to lead them to green pastures in exchange for sexual favors. She can be recognized for her inhuman nature by the fact that she has no back.

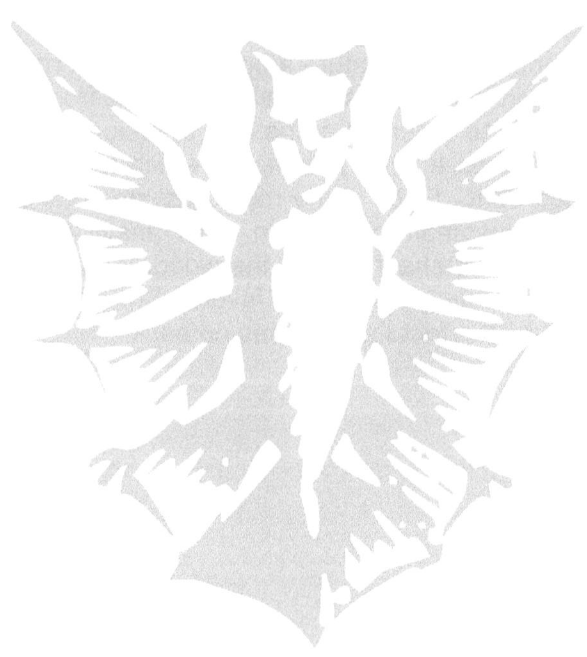

Bibliography

Barber, Paul. *Vampires, Burial, and Death.* Yale University Press, New Haven, CT: 1988.

Belanger, Michelle. *The Psychic Vampire Codex.* Weiser Books, Boston, MA: 2004

Belford, Barbara. *Bram Stoker.* Alfred A. Knopf, New York, NY: 1996

Bunson, Matthew. *The Vampire Encyclopedia.* Crown Publishers, New York, NY: 1993

Chen, Kaiguo. *Opening the Dragon Gate.* Thomas Cleary, trans. Tuttle Publishing: 1998.

Cleary, Thomas, trans. *Vitality, Energy, Spirit: A Taoist Sourcebook.* Shabhala Press, Boston, MA: 1991

Copper, Basil. *The Vampire in the Legend and Fact.* Citadel Press, New York, NY: 1973.

Dresser, Norine, *American Vampires: Fans, Victims, and Practitioners.* W. W. Norton Company, New York, NY: 1989

Eliade, Mircea. *Shamanism.* Williard Trask, trans. Bollingen Series, Princeton University Press, Princeton, NJ: 1964.

Guiley, Rosemary Ellen. *The Complete Vampire Companion.* MacMillan, New York, NY: 1994.

Jackson, Nigel. *The Compleat Vampyre.* Capall Bann Publishing, Berks, UK: 1995

Kalweit, Holger. *Dreamtime and Inner Space.* Shambhala Publications, Boston, MA: 1988

Kalweit, Holger. *Shamans, Healers, and Medicine Men.* Shambhala Publications, Boston, MA 2000

Konstantinos. *Vampires: the Occult Truth.* Llewellyn Publishing, St. Paul, MN: 1996

Longford, Elizabeth. *The Life of Byron.* Little, Brown & Co., Boston, MA: 1976

Mascetti, Manuela Dunn. *Vampire: the Complete Guide to the World of the Undead.* Viking Studio Books, New York, NY: 1992

McGann, Jerome, editor. *Lord Byron: the Major Works,* Oxford University Press: 2000

McNally, Raymond and Radu Florescu. *In Search of Dracula.* Houghton Mifflin Co., New York, NY: 1992

Midnight Sun. vols I—III. Michelle Belanger, editor. ISV publications, Hinckley, OH: 1994-1997

Murray, John. *Lord Byron and his Detractors.* Haskell House: 1971

Ramsland, Katherine. *Piercing the Darkness.* HarperPrism, New York, NY: 1998.

Rondina, Christopher. *Vampire Legends of Rhode Island.* Covered Bridge Press, North Attleborough, MA: 1997

Sebastian and Michelle Belanger. *The Vampyre Almanac 2000.* Sanguinarium Press, New York, NY: 2000

Senn, Harry. *The Were-Wolf and Vampire in Romania.* East European Monographs series. Columbia University Press, New York, NY: 1982

Wilhelm, Richard. *The Secret of the Golden Flower.* Harvest Books, New York, NY: 1962.

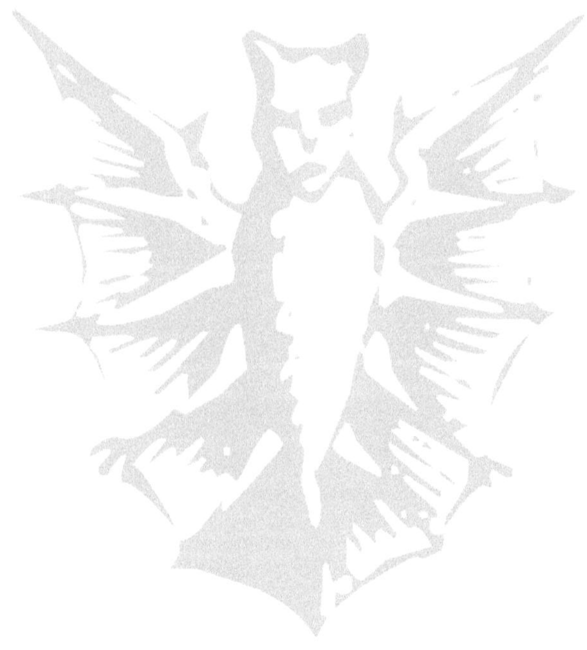

www.ingramcontent.com/pod-product-compliance
Ingram Content Group UK Ltd.
Pitfield, Milton Keynes, MK11 3LW, UK
UKHW041941190726
13854UKWH00004B/1718